P9-CAN-399

I WOULD
IF I COULD

Other Avon Camelot Books by
Betty Miles

JUST THE BEGINNING
MAUDIE AND ME AND THE DIRTY BOOK
THE REAL ME
THE TROUBLE WITH THIRTEEN

BETTY MILES is well known for her truthful and engaging novels for younger readers. A graduate of Antioch College, she has taught children's literature at Bank Street College of Education and was an editor of The Bank Street Readers. In addition to her writing, she works directly with school children, teachers, librarians, and parents concerned with children's reading and writing.

Like Patty Rader in I WOULD IF I COULD, Betty Miles spent many of her childhood summers in Ohio. She now lives with her husband in Rockland County, New York. They have three grown children.

Avon Books are available at special quantity discounts for bulk purchases for sales promotions, premiums, fund raising or educational use. Special books, or book excerpts, can also be created to fit specific needs.

For details write or telephone the office of the Director of Special Markets, Avon Books, Dept. FP, 1790 Broadway, New York, New York 10019, 212-399-1357.

I WOULD IF I COULD

Betty Miles

AN AVON CAMELOT BOOK

5th grade reading level has been determined by using the Fry Readability Scale.

AVON BOOKS
A division of
The Hearst Corporation
1790 Broadway
New York, New York 10019

Copyright © 1982 by Betty Miles
Published by arrangement with Alfred A. Knopf, Inc.
Library of Congress Catalog Card Number: 81-8458
ISBN: 0-380-63438-4

All rights reserved, which includes the right to
reproduce this book or portions thereof in any form
whatsoever except as provided by the U.S. Copyright Law.
For information address Alfred A. Knopf, Inc.,
201 East 50th Street, New York, New York 10022

The Alfred A. Knopf, Inc. edition contains the following
Library of Congress Cataloging in Publication Data:

Miles, Betty. I would if I could.
Summary: When the bicycle she's been longing for turns out to
be nothing like she expected, Patty is sick with disappointment.
Then the summer at her grandmother's teaches her several
valuable lessons. [1. Bicycles and bicycling—Fiction.
2. Friendship—Fiction] I. Title.
PZ.M594Pat   1982   [Fic]   81-8458
                                AACR2

First Camelot Printing, June 1983

CAMELOT TRADEMARK REG. U.S. PAT. OFF. AND IN
OTHER COUNTRIES, MARCA REGISTRADA, HECHO EN
U.S.A.

Printed in the U.S.A.

OPB 10 9 8 7 6 5

*Written with happy memories of
my grandmother, my aunt Grace, and my father,
and dedicated with love
to my aunt Nell and to my mother.*

❀

I WOULD
IF I COULD

❋
ONE

In her sleep, Patty felt the car slow down and stop.

She shifted on the seat. Her neck was sticky with sweat and her foot was asleep. Slowly, she opened her eyes and saw Dad beside her in the dark. For a moment, she didn't know why the two of them were here alone in the car on this hot night. Where was Mom? Suddenly she remembered. Mom was way back home in Pittsburgh. She and Dad were on their way to Clearwater, to Grandma's!

"Are we there yet?" Patty sat up and peered out at the unfamiliar street.

"Pretty near." Dad smiled down at her. "We're in St. Mary's."

"Oh, boy!" Patty came wide awake. St. Mary's, Ohio, was only an hour away from Clearwater. An hour from Grandma and from Aunt May, who lived with her. An hour from her very best friend in the whole world, Mary Alice Kallmeyer, and from the Staley twins around the corner. An hour from the surprise she had been waiting for so long. The long trip from Pittsburgh was almost over. She was practically *there*!

Dad wiped a handkerchief over his face. "I scream for ice cream," he said. "How about you?" He pointed across the street to the one bright window among the dark storefronts. The big white sign above it said ISALY'S in black letters.

"Yay, Isaly's!" That *proved* they were in Ohio. No other state in the U.S.A. had Isaly's ice-cream shops, but there was one in almost every Ohio town. Each summer, one of the first things Patty did in Clearwater was go downtown to Isaly's with Mary Alice for an ice-cream soda.

Patty pushed her door open. She climbed stiffly out of the car, hopping up and down on her prickly foot to wake it up, and looked around her. It was hard to believe she was standing here in St. Mary's, in the middle of the night, when only this morning she had been way back home in Pittsburgh. It made her feel like a character in an exciting radio serial. She imagined the announcer's introduction: "Patty stands bravely in the night," he would say, as organ music swelled behind his voice, "her eyes carefully surveying the deserted street. . . ."

She took Dad's hand and followed him toward the bright lights of Isaly's.

"It's *hot*." Patty pulled at her shorts where they stuck to the backs of her legs.

"It sure is," Dad said. "It must still be over ninety. Seems as though we picked the hottest day of 1938 to travel on." He squeezed her hand. "I was glad you could sleep through some of it."

"Did I sleep long?" asked Patty, feeling a little guilty. She had meant to stay awake the whole time, telling Dad jokes to keep him company on the long trip.

"You've been dead to the world since Zanesville," Dad said. "But don't worry. Your snores kept me awake."

"*Daddy!*" Dad always teased her about snoring, though Patty was positive she never did. The thing was, how could you prove it, if you were asleep?

Isaly's window was as bright as a movie screen, with the people inside moving across it like actors. Dad pulled the door open and a wave of cold air blew across Patty's bare arms and legs.

"You folks look like you've been traveling." The plump waitress smiled at them as they slid into the red leather booth.

"All the way from Pittsburgh," Dad told her.

"*That's* a trip." The waitress wiped their table a shiny black with her wet cloth. "And in this heat—" She smiled at Patty. "You tired out, hon?"

"Oh, no!" Patty tried to look wide awake, like an experienced traveler.

"Kept her eyes open the whole time." Dad winked at the waitress.

She laughed. "There's something about driving at night, just makes you sleepy," she said comfortably. "Now, what can I get you?"

5

"A strawberry soda and a mug of coffee," Dad ordered.

Isaly's was famous for its fancy ice-cream flavors, like frozen pudding and tutti-frutti. But Patty always stayed loyal to her favorite. "A vanilla soda, please," she said.

Across the room, the counterman lifted silver lids and dug out colored scoops of ice cream, squashing them down into cones. Cold steam flurried over his hands. Patty settled back against the booth, watching him happily. In the Clearwater Isaly's, she and Mary Alice usually sat on stools at the counter, to get served faster after the long hot walk downtown. *This* summer, she thought, maybe they could *ride* to Isaly's together. If only. . . .

"Can't you tell me what the surprise is now?" she begged Dad. "Now that we're almost there?"

"Then it wouldn't be a surprise," Dad said logically, smiling at her.

"I know, but—" Suddenly, Patty could hardly bear the suspense. Ever since Aunt May had written about the surprise that would be waiting for her in Clearwater, she had been trying not to pin her hopes on the one thing she wanted most. But now that they were so near, it was almost impossible to keep herself from hoping that the surprise would be—she crossed her fingers underneath the table—a *bike*. A blue one, with a white seat and a bell and a shiny wire basket. A bike so strong and safe, so steady on its fat balloon tires, that she could get right up onto it and ride.

It was awful not to know how. Patty was sure she was the only ten-year-old in the world who still couldn't ride a bike. She longed to be like the other kids at home who circled the school playground on their Elgins and American Flyers. But if one of them offered her a turn ("Come on, Patty, don't be a scaredy-cat") she would only shake her head.

She *was* a scaredy-cat. She had been one ever since that awful day in third grade when someone had pushed her suddenly from behind as she sat on a borrowed bike. The bike had rolled crazily down the hill behind school, with Patty unable to stop it, until it hit the cement curb of the playground pavement, and crashed. Patty had bounced off, bumping her head and scraping her leg open in a deep, raw gash. There was still a clump of small white scars on her leg to remind her of how the school nurse had dug out little bits of gravel, one by one. Patty would never forget the terror of falling, and the embarrassment of crying in front of all the kids. She had promised herself that she would never get on anyone's bike again until she could ride. But how could she learn, without a bike of her own to practice on?

Mom and Dad always seemed more worried about danger than other kids' parents, perhaps because Patty was their only child. At first, they had put off getting her a bike because of city traffic, and after the accident they were too upset even to consider it. "When you're older," they always said.

But now she *was* older, and not knowing how to

ride was worse. All this year, Patty had begged her parents for a bike. And from the way they had smiled at each other when Aunt May wrote about the surprise, she had been positive—almost positive—that Mom and Dad had agreed to let Aunt May buy her one this summer so she could learn to ride in Clearwater.

If I do get a bike, Patty promised herself as the waitress bustled toward them with a tray, I won't be a scaredy-cat. I'll get right up on it and *ride*.

"This'll cool you off." The waitress set Dad's mug of coffee and the sodas on the table. "Don't drink too fast, now," she warned in a friendly way. "You don't want to give yourself a headache."

She reminded Patty of Mom. "I wonder if Mom is missing us," she said, sucking the first cool mouthful of soda through her straw.

"Not right this minute," said Dad. "Mom's sure to be fast asleep by now."

It was funny to think of Mom sleeping back at home while Patty and Dad were wide awake in the St. Mary's Isaly's. It made her seem very far away. Patty remembered what she had said just before they drove off: "I'm going to miss you! But don't you spend any time missing me."

Patty was almost never homesick in the summers, except maybe on the very first day when Dad got into the car to drive back home without her. After that, she'd be having such a good time with Mary Alice—and sometimes with the Staley twins, too, when they wanted to be nice—that she'd almost forget about

Pittsburgh until the summer was over and it was time to go back home once more.

Dad set down his coffee cup and took out his wallet. "Ready to go?"

Patty spooned up the last frothy bubbles in the bottom of her glass while Dad paid the counterman and came back to slip a dime for the waitress beneath his mug. The waitress waved as they pushed through Isaly's door and walked into the hot night air. Patty climbed eagerly into the car and slammed her door shut.

The car moved slowly along the street, past dark stores and houses, until they reached the last empty lots of town.

"Good-bye, St. Mary's," Patty said, leaning back out of the window.

"Clearwater, here we come!" said Dad.

Patty sat straight in her seat, watching the road light up ahead of them in the headlights' beams. Little white bugs squashed against the windshield. On each side of the road, cornfields stretched off into the night. Patty looked at the dim circle of light on the dashboard where little numbers clicked and changed with the passing miles. They were going forty miles an hour! All of a sudden she could hardly wait to be there.

"John, Jacob, Jingleheimer Schmidt," she sang, to let some of her excitement out. "His name is my name, too."

Dad joined in. "Whenever we go out, the people always shout—"

"Here comes John, Jacob, Jingleheimer Schmidt!"

9

they finished together. "Da, da, da, *da,* da, da, da." They sang the song through three more times, whispering the verses more softly each time, until the "da's" came round and they could shout them out again.

"John, Jacob, Jingleheimer Schmidt" was one of Patty's favorite songs. She and Mary Alice liked to sing it over and over, until Mary Alice's big sister got aggravated and told them to shut up. Making Jeannie mad was part of the fun. Jeannie didn't like loud songs or Monopoly games or Orphan Annie radio programs the way Patty and Mary Alice did. Jeannie liked boys.

Patty wriggled on her seat, thinking of Jeannie and Mary Alice. Thinking about the bike. "I can't wait!" she said.

"How about a joke, to pass the time?" asked Dad.

"Okay." Patty loved to tell jokes. She had a whole bunch of good ones saved up to tell Mary Alice. Mary Alice didn't always *get* jokes, but at least she listened to them patiently. The kids back home never let you get to the funny part without interrupting.

"What did the mayonnaise say to the refrigerator?" Patty asked Dad.

Dad thought it over. That was a good thing about him—he always took jokes seriously. "Did it say, 'It's cold in here'?"

"No!" Patty shouted. "That wouldn't even be funny, Dad. Give up?"

"Guess I better."

"It said, 'Shut the door, I'm dressing,' " Patty yelled in triumph. "Get it? The mayonnaise was *dressing!*"

"That's a good one."

Dad slowed the car, pointing to a sign beside the road. "Look there," he said.

"Welcome to Clearwater," Patty read. "Oh, boy —we're here!" She leaned out of the window as Dad speeded up again. "Look, there's Miller's Dairy!" Familiar landmarks went by in the dark: the water tower, the canning factory, the tractor store. They passed big white farm houses with maple trees in front. Then, suddenly, the regular streets began. Dad slowed down to read the street signs, and turned onto Cedar Street.

"The Masonic Lodge!" Patty shouted out. "Caldwell School!" They were getting closer every minute. "Look, Dad, there's a new jungle gym in the park!"

At the far end of the park they turned and drove two blocks, past dark houses with only a few upstairs lights still on.

"The twins' house!" Patty yelled, just before Dad turned again, and then, "Elm Street!"

The familiar street looked almost magical in the dark. Patty could smell the phlox in someone's garden. Dad slowed down by the big white house on the corner with a porch across the front.

"Mary Alice's!" Patty shouted, not quite believing it and looking eagerly beyond it to the smaller house next door, where all the lights were blazing.

"Grandma's," she whispered happily.

Dad eased the car into Grandma's driveway, guiding it as carefully as though he were bringing a ship into port. The headlights lit up a bed of pink petunias beside the house. Dad turned off the engine and pulled up the brake. Then he leaned back and smiled at Patty. "Well, kid, we made it," he said. "We're here."

The screen door banged as Grandma and Aunt May ran down the porch steps, laughing and calling out.

Patty jumped out of the car and ran into Grandma's arms.

"Just look how she's grown!" Grandma squeezed her tight.

"Here you are!" said Aunt May, hugging her, too.

"Here I am," Patty said happily.

The long trip to Grandma's was over. Now the Clearwater summer had begun.

TWO

The minute Patty opened her eyes and saw the foot of the white metal bed against the yellow wallpaper roses, she knew. She was in Clearwater. And this was the day of the surprise.

She jumped out of bed, pushed back the curtain, and looked out. Beyond the garage, the Kallmeyers' grassy backyard, dappled with morning sunlight, sloped toward their house. And there, above the end of the side porch, was Mary Alice's window!

The shade was down. Mary Alice was a late sleeper. Sometimes Patty would have to go next door two or three different times, interrupting Mrs. Kallmeyer at her morning housecleaning, before she would find Mary Alice up and eating breakfast. Even then, it was always a long time before Mary Alice could play. Mrs. Kallmeyer made her eat very slowly, chewing each bite carefully to aid digestion, and drink up every drop of her morning Ovaltine, down to the grainy sludge at the bottom of the glass. Then Mrs. Kallmeyer would brush Mary Alice's pale yellow hair for one hundred strokes, until the back of her neck turned red, and twist it, clump by clump, around her finger into perfect fat curls.

At last Mary Alice would be set free, and the two of them would run out of the dark house to stand on the front walk in the sun, digging the toes of their sandals into the cracks as they argued happily about what to do first.

Patty let the curtain drop. She could hardly wait to see Mary Alice, but it was good Mary Alice was still asleep. By the time she woke up, Patty would know what the surprise was. And then, if it really was a bike, she could wheel it right over to the Kallmeyers' and show it off.

Quickly, she pulled on her playsuit and sandals, opened her bedroom door, and walked out into the hall. There was always a special smell to Grandma's house—a mixture of yeast and floor wax and Aunt May's Evening in Paris talcum powder. Aunt May's bed was already made, with the beautiful lady doll in flouncy skirts propped up on the pink chenille bedspread. Her dresser was covered with perfume bottles and jewelry boxes, and the frame of her mirror was full of post cards, invitations, and schedules of golf and tennis hours at the Club. Aunt May, who taught English at Clearwater High, filled her summer vacation with dates and activities. She was always rushing out of the house to do things with her friends.

Grandma's bedroom was plainer. There was a dark bed with a seersucker spread, a tall dresser, and a plain straight chair beside the sewing table, where a picture

14

of Patty and her mother was propped against a lamp. A large brown photograph of Grandma's husband— Mom's father and Patty's own grandfather, who died before she was born—hung in an oval gold frame over the bed.

It was so nice to be in this house again! Patty went into the bathroom, where the tub stood on legs and the white stand in the corner was piled with towels and sheets that had dried in the sun. She brushed her teeth, splashed water onto her face, and pulled off the rubber bands that dangled from her hair. She brushed her hair quickly, braided it into two loose pigtails, and put the rubber bands back on. Then she stared at her reflection in the medicine-chest mirror.

"I'm getting a bike," she told it, crossing her fingers one last time.

She ran down the stairs through the living room and dining room, and stopped still in the kitchen doorway.

Dad and Aunt May were eating breakfast at the table. Grandma turned around from the stove.

"Good morning!" She held her arms wide and Patty ran into them. "My, don't you look wide awake for somebody who was up till midnight!" Grandma gave her a squeeze. "Just see how she's grown, May. I can't get over it."

"*You* haven't changed at all, Grandma," Patty said. It was true. Grandma always looked the way a grandmother should. Like the grandmas in advertisements, she was short and plump. Her gray hair was done up in a bun, and her gold-rimmed glasses slipped down on her nose. She wore flower-printed house dresses with flower-printed aprons, trimmed in rickrack, on top of them.

Aunt May pulled a chair out. "Morning, hon. Sit down and have your cornflakes. We bought a new box just for you."

Patty kissed the top of Dad's head, hugged Aunt May, and slid into her chair.

"Did you sleep well?" Aunt May asked.

"Oh, yes." Patty drew a deep breath. "Aunt May, when am I going to see my surprise?"

"Now, Patty," Dad said. "Seems as though you could hold off a few minutes before you begin pestering your aunt." He winked at Aunt May. "You've got the whole summer for that."

"I know it." Patty sneaked a look out the window, but all she could see was the back porch and the steps and the car parked in the driveway. "But Aunt May said—"

"We'll see about it right after breakfast." Aunt May smiled knowingly at Dad. "It may take a few days for you to get used to it, Patty," she warned. "You mustn't expect—"

"I just hope to goodness she don't hurt herself on it," Grandma interrupted. "What would her mother say if anything happened to her?"

That *proves* it, Patty thought. It has to be a bike! She poured milk over her cornflakes and began to eat them quickly.

"Don't start worrying, now, Mama," Aunt May said. "She'll do just fine."

It always surprised Patty to hear Aunt May, or her own mother, call Grandma "Mama," as though they were still girls. Of course, they had been, once. The three sisters had grown up in this very house. Jean— Patty's mom—was the oldest. Aunt May was in the middle, and then came Aunt Flo, who was off in New York City this summer, going to school at Teachers College.

People always said that Patty was the spitting image of Aunt May, but in her heart Patty knew it wasn't true. Aunt May was tall and pretty, with golden brown hair that rippled over her ears in finger waves, while Patty was skinny and ordinary-looking, and her braids were just plain brown. Besides, Patty wasn't bouncy and full of personality like Aunt May. Or good at sports. Or popular. Aunt May was the most popular young teacher at Clearwater High. She had dozens of friends all over town, some of them her own students —big, self-confident kids like Buddy Engle, down the block, whose friendly teasing always embarrassed Patty. Every day Aunt May dashed off somewhere with her friends—to play golf or tennis at the Club, or to shop, or go to luncheons and bridge parties. Patty envied Aunt May's easy, assured manner. Patty was shy, and not very good at making friends. Except for Mary Alice, of course, but that didn't count. She'd never had to *make* friends with Mary Alice. They'd just always *been* friends, every single summer of their lives.

It was different with the Staley twins, whom she'd known almost as long. The twins acted more like the kids back home, giggly and superior. Sometimes Patty wondered if they only put up with her because Mary Alice made them. But why should she care? She knew that she, and not the twins, was Mary Alice's real best friend.

"Did Mary Alice know I was coming last night?" Patty scooped up the last spoonful of cornflakes.

"Did she *know*?" Aunt May laughed. "Mary Alice has been over here asking about you every day this week. She came by three times yesterday, just to see if you might have come early. She's going to be mighty excited when she wakes up this morning and sees the car in the driveway."

That's not all, Patty thought eagerly. Just wait till she sees the bike! She couldn't help feeling a little superior. Mary Alice had had the same old bicycle for years, a rusty hand-me-down that used to be Jeannie's. Patty promised herself that she'd be very generous this summer. She'd let Mary Alice use her bike anytime she wanted. Maybe she'd even let the Staley twins have turns on it, if they asked in a nice way and promised to be careful. The twins were really going to be surprised when they saw her riding her own bike.

If. Patty pushed her bowl away, almost dizzy with anxiety. It better be a bike, she thought. It *has* to be. Trying to sound natural, she looked at Aunt May. "Now is it time for the surprise?"

Aunt May smiled at Dad. "What do you say, Bob?"

"I say Patty's going to burst if she doesn't see it soon," Dad said, teasing.

"I just hope it's the right size," said Grandma.

Patty's heart sank. Was it a *dress*?

"She'll grow into it, Mama," Aunt May said.

Patty couldn't stand it. "Where *is* it?" she choked out.

"It's in the garage," Aunt May said, to Patty's relief. What else but a bike would be out there? "I'll go back and get it," she said. "When I call, you can bring Patty out on the steps to look." She winked at Dad. "I just can't wait to see her face when she sees it."

Patty squeezed her eyes shut as Aunt May went out. *Please*, she wished, let it be a bike. Behind her closed lids she could almost see it: a shiny blue bicycle, with fat white tires. Or maybe a red one. Red would be okay. It would be wonderful. Just wait till she showed Mary Alice!

"Ready!" Aunt May called from outside.

"Come with me, Dad." Patty grabbed his hand and pulled him out the door, her eyes still squeezed shut. All summer she had imagined herself standing here like this, waiting for the surprise to be revealed. Now that she was really here, she could hardly bear it. She wondered if she was going to faint. Blindly, she took a step forward, grabbed for the porch railing, and clung to it. Then she took a deep breath, opened her eyes, and looked down.

It was a bike! *But something was wrong with it!*

Patty hung giddily to the railing and stared down in dismay.

Aunt May was smiling up at her, holding a bicycle by the handlebars. But what kind of bicycle was this?

It wasn't blue, or even red, but a dark muddy green—and it was so big and thin that Patty wondered how anyone could balance on it. It had narrow wheels and a narrow seat and no basket. The handlebars seemed to be set onto it backwards, and the pedals were tiny. Patty gripped the railing, staring down. She could hardly believe her eyes. The bike was enormous—it must be twice as big as she was. It was the strangest, scariest-looking bicycle she had ever seen in her life. It was *horrible*.

"Well, what do you say?" Aunt May called cheerfully.

Patty couldn't say anything.

Behind her, Dad cleared his throat.

"I don't know," Grandma began. "I told you, May, I said, 'That's an awful big bike for a little girl.'"

Patty swallowed hard. In the bright sunshine, the bike looked like a giant insect, with curving handlebar feelers and a thin, glittering body.

"It's an Imperial," Aunt May was saying proudly. "The first real English bicycle in Clearwater. Maybe in all of Ohio!" She patted a thin green fender. "They say it's the strongest, safest, best-designed bike in the world," she explained to Dad. Then she smiled at Patty. "How's *that* for a surprise?"

Patty tried to answer. Nothing came out.

"I only wish your mother could see your face right now," said Aunt May happily.

Patty wondered what her face must look like. Slowly, she forced her mouth into a smile. Then, shaking with disappointment, she made herself run down the steps to hug Aunt May.

"Oh, boy," she choked out, trying hard not to sob. "Oh, boy, Aunt May. It's just what I wanted—a *bike*!"

❋

THREE

Before Patty could protest, Dad lifted her up and set her on the bicycle seat. The front wheel wobbled as she clung to the handlebars, trying not to look at the sharp little stones on the driveway far beneath her that would grind into her bare knees if she fell.

"Careful!" Grandma called from the steps. "Don't let her fall!"

The thin seat cut sharply into Patty's behind. She shifted her weight and the bike tilted suddenly under her.

"Steady, now." Dad tightened his grip on her waist and straightened the front wheel.

"Put your feet on the pedals," said Aunt May.

Cautiously, Patty reached down with one foot, but the pedal whirled away as she touched it, and the front wheel turned sharply to the right.

"Daddy!" she cried out, squeezing the handgrips in her sweaty palms. If the bike was this tippy now, with Dad holding it up, how could she ever manage to balance it by herself? How was she going to learn to *ride*?

"Hang on. Here we go!" Dad began to push the bike down the driveway.

"Daddy!" It seemed to be rolling out from under her. "*Stop!*"

"Look out," called Grandma. "Hold her tight, Bob."

"She's all right, Mama." Aunt May looked anxious. "She just has to get the feel of it."

I'll *never* get the feel of it, Patty told herself grimly as Dad pulled the bike to a stop.

"Don't worry, kid," he whispered into her ear. "It's bound to feel strange at first. But just wait. In a couple of days, you'll be pedaling up and down Elm Street like an expert."

Patty nodded miserably, knowing he was wrong.

A car slowed down in the street. "Hi there, Miss Schultz," the driver called. Patty looked up nervously. It was Buddy Engle, the high-school boy from down the street. Why did he have to come around right now? She tried to hide her face behind Dad's shoulder, but it was too late.

"Hey there, Patty!" Buddy called. "Glad to see you back. Where'd you get the snazzy bike?"

Could he tell she didn't know how to ride it? Embarrassed, Patty raised one hand in what she hoped looked like a casual wave, putting it down fast as the handlebars swung sideways.

"Daddy, help me down," she said urgently.

"Careful." Dad grabbed her waist as she slid awkwardly off the seat, scraping her leg on the pedal.

In the street, Buddy honked and drove off. He was probably laughing at her. Patty wanted to cry.

"Well, what do you think of it?" Aunt May asked. "The man down at the bike store says English bikes are the very best in the world," she said to Dad. "You can go home and tell Jean that Patty's starting out right." She stroked the front fender. "And she won't grow out of this one. It'll last a lifetime."

Patty's heart sank.

"It may be a little harder to learn on than some bikes," Aunt May went on. "It took me a while to get the hang of it when I tried it out. But we'll take it slow, practice every day." She gave Patty an encouraging smile. "I bet you're going to be the fastest rider in Clearwater. Mary Alice won't be able to keep up with you."

Mary Alice! Quickly, Patty looked over at her window. The shade was still down. At least Mary Alice hadn't been watching. But she probably knew all about the bicycle already. Like Buddy Engle. Like half the people in Clearwater. The Staley twins! The full horror of it began to sink in. She was stuck with this awful bike for her whole visit. For her whole life!

Dad was looking at the seat. "I think this may be a little high for Patty."

"Oh, it's adjustable," Aunt May said. "The instruction book shows how."

She ran inside and came out with a booklet, which she gave to Dad. Patty peered at it over his arm. There was a picture of a bike like hers on the cover, with the words "Streamlined Elegance" beneath it.

"What does 'streamlined' mean?" Patty asked.

"It means a machine that's made to be sleek and

fast, without extra weight to slow it down." Dad opened the book. "Well, look here: 'By appointment to His Majesty,' it says." He turned to Patty. "That means the King of England has a bike like yours, kid."

"Oh." Patty wondered how the King would learn to ride. Who would teach him? What would they say if he fell off?

Dad was studying a diagram of the bicycle. "Would you like me to work on the seat now?" he asked Aunt May.

"Oh, no thanks, Bob," she said. "Patty and I can do that ourselves." She looked at her watch. "I'd do it now, but I've promised to meet Ruth Gebhardt out at the Club at ten. The summer golf tournament's going on," she apologized. "I'll be out there most of today and tomorrow. It's a pity it had to come right at the start of your visit, Patty. I won't have much time to help you with the bike until it's over."

"That's okay," Patty said quickly, trying to forget that she'd promised herself to be *riding* this very day. "I don't need to start learning right away."

"Well." Dad laid his hand on Patty's shoulder as Aunt May dashed inside. "I guess it's about time for me to be on my way."

"Now?" Patty was startled. "Can't you stay just a little bit longer?"

"Mom's expecting me," Dad said gently. "And I've got a long trip ahead. Without any company." He winked at her. "I'll miss your snores on the way back."

"Daddy!" Patty tried to laugh, but only a hiccup came out.

25

"Don't let that bike worry you, kid," he said. "Just between you and me," he lowered his voice, "I think your aunt might have picked out a smaller bike for a beginner. But she wanted you to start right out with the best. It's a good, sturdy bike," he added. "And you're a good, sturdy kid. You'll master it. Remember the Little Engine—'I think I can, I think I can—'"

Patty nodded.

"Well—" Dad held out his hand and drew her toward the steps. She climbed up slowly behind him, trying not to look down at the bike. When he was gone, she'd be here alone, with *it*.

In the kitchen, Grandma gave Dad a shoe box tied with string. "I hope this is enough lunch," she said. "There's bologna-and-cheese sandwiches, and peaches, and some of my date bars—"

"Sounds like enough for an army," Dad said. "And I'm leaving my army behind." He winked at Patty. "I'll just go and get my things."

Grandma looked at Patty's face. "Come here and sit on my lap a minute." She pulled Patty to her. "It's real nice to have our little girl back again," she said, smoothing Patty's hair. "We'll have lots of good times together, you wait and see. And don't you worry about that old bicycle," she went on comfortingly. "I told your aunt. 'May,' I said, 'you let Patty take her time with that thing. Give her a chance to get settled, first. It's no use pushing her.'"

"Yeah." Patty snuggled against Grandma. It felt good to sit on her lap again, even though she was getting a little too big to fit there comfortably. She leaned her head on Grandma's plump bosom, letting herself—just for a minute—feel like a cozy baby. The trouble was, she didn't want Grandma, or Aunt May, or anyone else, to think she *was* a baby. That's what I am, though, she thought unhappily as Grandma's heart beat softly beneath her. A scaredy-cat baby who can't even ride a bike. A sigh she couldn't hold back came out of her.

Grandma squeezed her tight. "You know what might happen while you're here?" she confided. "Your grandmother might just win twenty-five dollars in a contest! What would you think of that?"

"Twenty-five *dollars!*" Patty sat up. "Boy, Grandma! What kind of a contest is it?" Grandma was always sending entries in to contests she heard about on the radio. Once, she won a packet of marigold seeds for a jingle about soap flakes, but she had never won anything else.

"It's a flour-naming contest," Grandma said. "Whatever name they pick, they're going to put on every bag of flour they sell, all over the state of Ohio. And I just think my name might win."

"What name is it?" Patty asked eagerly.

"It's a name that came to me all of a sudden," Grandma said, "one day about two weeks ago. I baked up a batch of muffins—the prettiest muffins you'd ever want to see. And when I took them out of the oven, I said to May, 'Just look at the crust on these muffins,' I said. 'It's like gold.' That's when the name came to me." She paused dramatically.

"*What* name?" Patty asked again.

"Golden Crust!" Grandma said. "Golden Crust Flour. What do you think of that?"

"I think it's a swell name!" Patty said. "If I were the judge, *I'd* pick it. Not just because you're my grandma, either. Even if I didn't know you, I would."

"Well, cross your fingers," Grandma said as Dad came into the kitchen with his overnight bag in his hand.

"Guess it's time to hit the road." He squeezed Patty's shoulder gently.

"Be sure and stop for a good rest at lunchtime, now," Grandma said.

"And do be sure to give Jean our love." Aunt May came into the kitchen wearing her golf culottes and a green visor hat.

"I promise to do both." Dad kissed Aunt May's cheek and gave Grandma a hug. Then he took Patty's hand. "Now, don't let this kid do anything I wouldn't do."

"Daddy!" Patty followed him to the door, holding onto his shirt sleeve as he went down the steps.

Grandma and Aunt May watched from the back porch as they carried Dad's overnight bag to the car and pushed it inside the trunk.

Dad slammed it shut. "Well, kid—" He held out his arms.

Patty hugged him tightly around the chest, pressing her face into his shirt.

Dad squeezed her tight. Then he opened the car door and slid behind the wheel. "Show that bicycle who's boss," he said.

"I will." Patty felt an ache rising in the back of her throat.

Dad turned the key and the engine started up. Slowly, the car rolled down the driveway.

"Good-bye, Daddy." Patty walked beside it, her hand on the fender. "Good-bye," she said again. The car backed into the street.

"Have a good summer," Dad called through the window.

"*Good-bye!*" Patty ran down the sidewalk, waving, as the car picked up speed.

Dad waved back, honking the horn as he turned the corner.

Then he was gone.

❋
FOUR

Long after the car had vanished, Patty stood on the curb, staring down the empty street. Morning sunlight fell through the elm trees, lighting up streams of dust specks in the air and making bright splotches on the pavement. The street was lined with small white houses like Grandma's, half-hidden behind vine-covered porches. The Kallmeyers' big house on its wide double lot stood imposingly on the corner. Elm Street looked exactly the same, Patty thought. Standing here was like standing in a memory of all the other mornings, as far back as she could remember, waiting for Mary Alice to wake up so the long summer day could begin.

But this day was so different from those other days! Horribly different from the way she'd dreamed it would be when she sat in Isaly's last night. That dream had vanished as totally as Dad. He'd be way out at the edge of town by now, heading back over the road they'd traveled yesterday: back to St. Mary's and Zanesville, and way on back to Pittsburgh and to Mom. Leaving Patty here, with the funny ache in her throat, and that awful bicycle standing by the house behind her. *Her* bicycle.

"*Patty!*"

Mary Alice, waving wildly, was running across her yard.

"Mary *Alice!*" Patty started running, too.

They hurtled together, laughing, grabbing at each other to keep from falling down. Then they backed off and stared at each other almost shyly.

Mary Alice was wearing a polka-dotted playsuit that Patty had never seen before, but otherwise she looked the same—plumpish and pink-cheeked, with her hair in perfect sausage curls and a grin that showed the space between her two front teeth.

"Boy, Patty," she said, breaking the spell. "I just couldn't wait till you got here!"

"Me, either." For a minute, Patty forgot about the bike. *This* was what she'd been waiting for.

"Guess what?" Mary Alice started right in. "Jeannie has a boyfriend!" She giggled. "Wait till you see him. He has big ears and a long skinny neck, but Jeannie thinks he looks like Gary Cooper." She made a face. "His name's Donald. Old Donald Duck Barnes. He's always hanging around, sitting on the porch swing, waiting for Jeannie to come out."

"What do they do?" Patty asked eagerly.

"Nothing," said Mary Alice with disgust. "Except make eyes at each other. You should hear Jeannie. Whenever Donald says anything, she says, 'Ooh, Donald!'" She tilted her head back and grinned stupidly. "Ooh, Donald!"

31

Patty laughed.

"Guess what?" Mary Alice went on. "The twins went to Columbus, to their grandmother's."

"They did?" Patty's spirits rose. That meant she'd have Mary Alice all to herself! And the twins wouldn't be hanging around to make fun of the bike. "For how long?"

"Till Labor Day."

"I guess I won't even see them this year, then." Patty tried not to sound too pleased. After all, the twins were Mary Alice's *next*-best friends.

"Guess what they got for their birthday," Mary Alice asked hesitantly.

"*What?*" Patty was afraid to guess.

"New bikes. Blue ones. Twenty-eight-inch Elgins. You should see them, Patty. They're really swell." Mary Alice looked uncomfortable.

"The lucky ducks!" Patty burst out. Myrna and Erna had all the luck! Just being twins in the first place, with their special rhyming names, and wearing cute twin outfits and having people make a fuss over them, pretending not to know who was who. And getting to play with Mary Alice all year round. It was so unfair that they should get new Elgins, on top of everything. "I wish *I* was them!" Patty said bitterly.

Mary Alice looked sympathetic. "Did you see the surprise your aunt got you yet?"

Patty swallowed. "Yeah. Did you?"

"I saw it yesterday, when she brought it home." Mary Alice kicked at the grass with her sandal. "I never saw a bike like it before," she said. "I guess in England it's a real popular kind," she added quickly.

"I know, but this is *here!*" Patty countered. "Nobody here wants a bike like that." She eyed Mary Alice defiantly. "I bet you wouldn't!"

"Well . . ." Mary Alice wasn't any good at lying. "I already have a bike," she said after a minute.

"Yeah, and you already know how to ride, too. How would you like to have to learn on *that?*"

"Oh, Patty!" Mary Alice looked surprised. "Didn't you learn how yet? You said you would. You said you'd get the kids at school to teach you."

"Well, I didn't." Patty had never been able to come right out and tell Mary Alice what it was like with the kids back home. It was too hard to explain that she didn't really have the kind of friends who'd be patient enough to help you learn to ride.

For years, Mary Alice had tried to teach Patty on her bike. But that had never worked. Both girls were always too afraid that Mrs. Kallmeyer would find out. Mrs. Kallmeyer had what she called her "principles," and one of them was that Jeannie and Mary Alice should never let other kids use their bikes. "I can't accept the responsibility," Mrs. Kallmeyer always said, pressing her hand to her heart as though she was already mourning a run-over child and a smashed bicycle.

"Well, listen, Patty," Mary Alice said earnestly. "I bet you can learn this summer, if you practice every day. Look what a good teacher your aunt is. She'll help you. I will, too." She touched Patty's arm. "No kidding. You'll probably catch on fast, now that you have your own bike to learn on."

"I'll *never* learn." Patty squelched the little flicker of hope that rose up at Mary Alice's confident tone.

"Well, anyway," said Mary Alice. "You don't have to worry about it right this minute. You just got here. There's lots of other stuff to do. Hey, guess what?" She grabbed Patty's arm and pulled her across the lawn toward the front sidewalk. "Want to see something funny?" She pointed at the side of the telephone pole. "Look!"

Patty stared at the strange chalk marks on the pole. They reminded her of the Egyptian hieroglyphics in a geography book. The little lines and circles looked like writing, but she couldn't read them.

"What do they mean?" she asked.

"I don't know." Mary Alice looked serious. "I think it could be some kind of spy code. Remember last year when Orphan Annie got mixed up with that bunch of spies? *They* wrote messages in chalk."

"Yeah, but why would spies want to come to Clearwater?"

"Spies go anywhere," said Mary Alice firmly. "Besides, there's been some strange men that nobody knows walking around town. The twins said—"

"Why, here's *Patty*!" Mrs. Kallmeyer called from the porch. "Come here and say hello, dear."

Patty walked over to the porch and let Mrs. Kallmeyer kiss her.

"Isn't it wonderful to see you!" Mrs. Kallmeyer

stood back to look her up and down. "Why, I just can't believe how you've grown!"

Patty stared at her feet. She was always embarrassed by these inspections. Each year, it seemed as though everyone—the neighbors, Grandma and Aunt May's friends, practically the whole congregation at the Presbyterian Church—had to tell her how much she'd grown. It was fun to surprise Grandma, but she felt shy when other people looked her over. It always made her wonder if her neck was clean.

"Come in and have a nice glass of Kool-Aid." Mrs. Kallmeyer held the screen door open.

Patty and Mary Alice walked into the dark house, where the drapes were already pulled shut against the heat. Patty looked around the living room. It was stuffed with heavy furniture and knicknacks, and it smelled faintly of Lysol and Mr. Kallmeyer's cigars. The room was as comfortably familiar to Patty as Grandma's. She and Mary Alice had spent endless mornings here, cutting out paper dolls and reading books in the dim yellow light of the shaded lamps while Jeannie played popular songs on the piano and the hot sun beat down outside.

"Well, hi there, Patty!" Jeannie came out of the kitchen in her housecoat, with her hair clumped over her head in rag rollers. She stared at Patty, pretending to be astonished.

"Look at *her*," she said. "Will you just look at how she's grown!" She laughed an adult kind of laugh.

"Hi, Jeannie," Patty said awkwardly, feeling like a baby in front of her.

35

"I hear you got a snazzy new bike," Jeannie said. "I guess nobody in Clearwater's going to keep up with *you*."

Patty looked helplessly at Mary Alice. Did everyone know?

"Hey, Jeannie," Mary Alice interrupted quickly. "Want me to call up Donald Barnes and tell him to come over to see your glamorous hairdo?"

"Mama, make her shut up." Jeannie started for the stairs, patting her curlers.

"I declare, Mary Alice," Mrs. Kallmeyer said reproachfully, leading the girls into the kitchen. "Some *other* child would speak nice to her own sister."

Mrs. Kallmeyer was always holding up the example of a nonexistent "other child" who would behave better than Mary Alice.

"Well, Patty," she went on, sitting them down at the kitchen table. "You surely picked a hot time to visit. It's a shame you girls can't go swimming in this heat."

"Why can't we?" asked Patty, surprised. Every summer she and Mary Alice, and sometimes the twins, went out to the town pool with their suits in rolled-up towels and money for orange pop in their coin purses. They would stay there all afternoon, jumping in and out of the chlorine-green water, paddling and splashing and fooling around.

"Oh, didn't your grandmother tell you?" Mrs. Kallmeyer put jelly glasses of purple Kool-Aid in front of them. "They've closed the pool." She sighed. "Because of the terrible polio epidemic up to Toledo.

36

Five little children already crippled for life," she said solemnly. "And who knows how many others sick, or even about to die—"

"But why would they close *our* pool?" Patty knew how terrible polio was. There were newspaper stories about it that Mom and Dad shook their heads over sadly. But if nobody in Clearwater was sick. . . . "Nobody here got it, did they?" she asked anxiously.

"Not yet, thank the Lord," said Mrs. Kallmeyer. "But you can't be too careful, what with those awful germs going around, turning up who knows where. The only safe thing is to keep away from crowds. That's why they shut the pool down for the season." She sighed again. "You'd think that if they can figure out how to send voices over the air all the way from New York City to Clearwater, Ohio, *somebody'd* figure out a way to protect little children from polio germs."

"Anyway, Dad fixed up the lawn sprinkler for us," Mary Alice put in, draining her glass. "It's fun to play in. The twins and I went in it every day before they left."

"Yes, you can have a real nice time with that," Mrs. Kallmeyer said. "To tell the honest truth, I can't say I feel too bad that they closed the pool down. I always did worry you'd catch *something* out there. A place like that's bound to be full of germs."

Mary Alice pushed her chair back. "Want to play Monopoly, Patty?"

"Sure." Patty got up, too. "Thanks for the Kool-Aid, Mrs. Kallmeyer."

"You're welcome, dear." Mrs. Kallmeyer looked at Mary Alice and waited.

"Thanks, Mom," Mary Alice mumbled. She tugged at Patty's arm. "Come on."

"Mary Alice!" Mrs. Kallmeyer's voice had a scolding sound. "Some *other* child would remember to clear the table for her mother."

"Oh, yeah." Mary Alice ducked back to gather up the glasses and rinse them out in the sink, the way some other child would have done without having to be reminded.

"Let's play on the porch," she said, spreading the dishrag neatly across the sink.

Patty followed her out of the house. By now the sun was high, but only little splashes of sunlight fell onto the porch table through the thick lilacs in front of the railing.

Patty sank onto the flowered glider as Mary Alice pulled a shell-shaped metal chair to the table and unfolded the Monopoly board between them.

"You still want the battleship?" she asked.

"Yep." The battleship was Patty's good luck piece.

Mary Alice set the battleship on the board beside her own favorite, the top hat, and began to deal out the money.

Patty settled back on the glider, which squeaked out its same old springy tune. "Hey, Mary Alice," she asked eagerly. "What did the mayonnaise say to the refrigerator?"

"I give up." Mary Alice always gave up without even trying to guess a joke. "What?"

38

"It said, 'Shut the door, I'm dressing!' " Patty shouted.

"I don't get it," said Mary Alice, as Patty had known she would.

"See, the mayonnaise was *dressing*," Patty explained, a wave of contentment sweeping over her. Here she was at last, on Mary Alice's front porch, with the game just beginning and the whole long day to play it in. Carefully, she straightened the cards in the Community Chest pile and arranged the little wooden houses and hotels in rows beside the board. Pushing thoughts of the bicycle firmly to the back of her mind, she studied the empty Monopoly board with its yellow and purple and green streets waiting to be filled. Park Place, Boardwalk, Pennsylvania Avenue. . . .

Oh, boy, she thought happily, tossing the dice to see who would go first. At least the best things in Clearwater have stayed exactly the same.

FIVE

The mailman was coming up the street, crisscrossing from side to side. Patty went out to wait for him. Maybe by now there would be a letter from Mom.

The bicycle stood by the steps, where it had been standing ever since Dad left four days ago. Even though Aunt May had lowered the seat, it still looked awfully tall. Its spokes and handlebars glinted ominously in the bright sun.

Patty walked around it, trying not to think of the promise she'd made to herself in the St. Mary's Isaly's. *If I get a bike, I won't be a scaredy-cat. I'll get right up on it and ride.*

She blinked, watching the mailman walk away from the Engles' box. It wasn't *her* fault she hadn't kept her promise. If she had known what kind of a bike it would turn out to be, she would never have thought she could ride it. She kicked at a little stone in the driveway, remembering what Dad had said about the Little Engine. They ought to have another book, she told herself bitterly, called *The Little Engine That*

40

Couldn't. That Little Engine would say, "I would if I could, but I can't."

Sighing, Patty walked across the street to meet the mailman, who had been bringing her letters in Clearwater ever since she was too young to read them by herself.

"Hi, there, honey." The mailman shuffled through a handful of letters. "Let's see what we've got here. A postcard for your aunt, a letter for your Grandma—" He held out an envelope, pretending to study the address. "Well, now, here's one for a Miss Patty Rader, 27 Elm Street. I wonder who that could be?"

"That's *me!*" Patty reached out eagerly, recognizing Mom's familiar handwriting on the envelope.

"So that's who you are!" The mailman wiped his face with a handkerchief, looking over Patty's shoulder. "Looks like this summer we'll have to call you Patty Rader the Rider," he said, jerking his thumb at the bicycle. "Say, how'd you let that friend of yours get away without you?" he teased. "I saw her riding lickety-split down Central Avenue a little while ago."

"She went to the store for her mother," Patty said shortly. What business was it of his, anyway?

"Well, see you tomorrow." The mailman waved and went on toward the Kallmeyers'.

Patty sat on the steps and opened her envelope slowly. It was funny how getting a letter from Mom made her suddenly seem much farther away.

"Dear Patty," the letter began. "How are you? Dad and I are fine. We think about you lots, and miss you

41

lots. *You're* missing a real hot spell in Pittsburgh. I'm glad you're out of this hot city. Have you gone swimming yet?"

She would have to tell Mom that the Clearwater pool was closed. She'd mention it very casually, so Mom wouldn't worry.

"I know you and Mary Alice must be having a wonderful time together," Mom went on.

Patty laid the letter down. If only it weren't for the bike! Except for that, they *were* having a wonderful time. It was more fun than ever with Mary Alice this summer, because the twins weren't around to butt in. The two of them had spent their days doing all the things Patty had looked forward to: cutting out paper-doll clothes; playing jacks and Old Maid and Monopoly; bouncing up and down on the seesaw in the park and skipping down the sidewalk in perfect step with their arms around each other. They studied paddle balls and jump ropes at Woolworth's, and ordered ice-cream sodas at Isaly's before the long walk home. Then, lying head to foot on the couch at one of their houses, they would re-read the books they read each summer and already knew by heart.

In the late afternoons, they sprawled on the rug in front of the Kallmeyers' big Motorola radio and listened to the adventures of Little Orphan Annie, who was chasing pirates in the Amazon. After supper, when the days faded into hazy twilight, they ran across the wet grass on the Kallmeyers' side lawn, shrieking as cool spray from the sprinkler pelted over them. And when the real dark fell, they crept quietly

42

onto the porch steps to peek at Jeannie and Donald Barnes on the glider, giggling helplessly to themselves. Only when Grandma and Mrs. Kallmeyer insisted ("Mary Alice, this is the very last time I intend to call you!") did they finally say good-night and go inside.

If only it weren't for the bicycle, it would all be so perfect! Patty picked up her letter again, bracing herself for what Mom would say.

"Daddy told me how excited you were about the bicycle," the letter went on. "Isn't it something to have a bike that comes from England! It's fun to imagine you riding up and down Elm Street. (I won't tell you to be careful because I know you will be.)

"How are Grandma and Aunt May? Give them each a kiss from me. And here's a big one for my bike rider. I hope you're having the best visit ever. Are the Staley twins there? Lots of love, Mother."

Patty stuffed the letter in her pocket and went inside, glad that Grandma had gone out to see Mrs. Engle before the mailman came. She needed time by herself to answer Mom. She went upstairs to her room and took out the Mickey Mouse stationery Mom had given her before she left. Then she went downstairs again, took a pencil from the drawer of the kitchen table, and sat down to write.

What was she going to say?

She couldn't tell Mom and Dad how scared she was of the bicycle. Or how hard it was to put off lessons with Aunt May, or to explain to Mary Alice why she wasn't even trying to learn. She couldn't tell them how much Grandma's stories about children who fell off their bikes and got concussions or broken bones worried her. She wouldn't want them to know how sad she felt when packs of kids raced their bikes down Elm Street, shouting happily at each other, or how wistfully she looked through Isaly's window at the bicycles parked outside. She couldn't say how bad she'd felt this morning when Mrs. Kallmeyer needed something from the store and Mary Alice had ridden off to get it, leaving her behind.

Patty picked up her pencil and wrote "Dear Mom and Dad" beneath Mickey's smiling face. "How are you?" she went on. "I am fine. Mom's letter just came. I was very glad to get it. It is hot here, too. We can't go swimming because the pool is closed. But Mr. Kallmeyer fixed up the sprinkler for us. It is fun. Mary Alice and I are having lots of fun."

She paused, staring at the page. It was only half full.

"It is too bad," she went on, "but the Staley twins aren't here. They went to see their grandmother in Columbus."

There was still a lot of empty space. "Aunt May is out at the Club now. Grandma is down at the Engles'," she wrote, in large letters. "They will be back," she added.

She couldn't think of what else to write. "Well, I guess I better stop now," she finished up. "Mary Alice will be coming over soon."

She filled the rest of the page with big X's and wrote "Love, Patty" at the bottom. Then she read her letter through. It sounded okay, but she knew Mom and

Dad would wonder why she hadn't said anything about the bike.

"P.S.," she added, in small letters, below her name. "The bicycle is very nice."

Writing the lie felt awful. Patty sealed the letter quickly, addressed the envelope, and set it on the shelf above the sink. Then she looked outside to see if Mary Alice was riding back up the street. There was no sign of her. Without meaning to, Patty glanced down at the bike. It was just *standing* there, as usual.

That stupid bike! She'd show it. Angrily, Patty ran down the steps and grabbed the handlebars. Holding on tightly, she shoved the bike along the driveway. She might not be able to ride it, but at least she could make it *move*.

The bike rolled bumpily beside her. She guided it awkwardly, holding it far enough away so the pedal wouldn't hit her leg. The wheels seemed to want to go in different directions. Patty straightened the front one as it tipped to the right. The bike picked up speed and almost got away from her. She pulled back hard to slow it down before it could bounce over the curb and into the street. Then she dragged the bike into a wide turn and began to shove it back up the driveway. It was easier, going this direction. The bike rolled straight ahead. Maybe if somebody drove past right now they might think she had just come home from a long ride. Cautiously, she let go of one hand grip and grabbed the back of the seat. It was easier to guide it this way. She turned the bike toward the steps. This wasn't so terrible! If she could keep it straight like this

45

by herself, she could probably keep her balance the next time Aunt May pushed her. . . .

"Hey, Patty!"

Patty wheeled around to see Buddy Engle coming toward her on the sidewalk. Startled, she let the bike slip out of her hands. It fell to the ground with its handlebars wound around her legs.

Red-faced, Patty tugged at the bike, trying to free herself.

"Gee, I'm sorry. I didn't mean to scare you." Buddy bent over and untangled the bike. He set it straight, holding it steady with one hand. "This is some machine," he said, whirling the wheel around with the other. "You're a lucky kid, you know that? I wouldn't mind having a fancy bike like this." He looked at Patty. "Say, how about if I give it a little test run, out in the street?"

"Okay." Annoyed, Patty stepped back. He had some nerve!

Buddy threw one leg over the bike, set his foot on the pedal, and pushed off with the other. Wobbling unsteadily for a moment, he turned the wheel straight and bounced the bike off the curb into the street, swinging out in a wide, easy arc.

"Hey, this thing really goes!" he shouted back over his shoulder. "Whoopee!" He was halfway down the block already, crouched over the handlebars and pedaling hard.

Patty stood on the curb watching him go. Who did he think he was, anyway, grabbing the bike away from her like that? Didn't he know he'd made her fall?

"Darn you, Buddy!" she called after him, but of course he couldn't hear her. Only a faint shout floated behind him as he swooped around the corner of Elm Street and was gone.

"*Patty!* Guess what!"

Patty spun around.

Mary Alice came cutting across her lawn on her bicycle, pedaling furiously, making a track in the grass that Mrs. Kallmeyer would scold her for later. Breathless, she pulled up short in front of Patty and jumped off.

"Guess what!" she burst out excitedly. "The twins came back!"

SIX

"They did?" Patty's heart sank. "How *come*?"

"There's a polio epidemic in Columbus," Mary Alice reported dramatically, straddling her bike. "Five kids got it already. So the twins had to come home. They just called up."

"Did *they* get it?" Patty tried not to sound hopeful. But if the twins were sick in bed, they couldn't spoil things too much.

"They're okay," said Mary Alice. "But this boy who lives next door to their grandmother's friend got it. He goes to their grandmother's church. The twins saw him there last Sunday, and the next day he was in the *hospital*."

Mary Alice seemed so impressed that Patty was exasperated. "What's so great about knowing a boy who got polio? Aren't the twins even sorry for him?" She had a sudden flash of hope. "Hey, I bet that means the twins could be contagious!"

"They're not," Mary Alice replied, setting her bike on its kickstand. "Their mom said. You aren't contagious unless somebody in your family gets it, or if a person who has it sneezes all over you, or kisses you or something." She giggled. "Anyway, this boy sang in the church choir. He didn't sit near the twins."

"Yeah, but he must have had to walk past their pew in the processional, and the recessional. Some of his germs could have blown onto them."

"Patty!" Now Mary Alice looked irritated. "You have to do more than just walk *past* a person to give them polio. The twins' own *mother* ought to know. Anyway, Mom said it's okay for them to come over if they wash first, and cover their mouths when they sneeze."

"Oh." Patty gave up. That meant this was probably the last day in the whole visit she'd be alone with Mary Alice!

"Well, what do you want to do now?" she asked, to make the most of it. "Want to come up to my room and cut out paper dolls?"

Mary Alice hesitated. "I better not. The twins said they were coming over."

Couldn't they even wait one day before they came butting in? "Well, then your mom can tell them to come over *here*," Patty said reasonably. "Come on, Mary Alice. Let's not waste time just standing here. Let's go do something."

Mary Alice looked embarrassed. "The thing is—"
"*What?*"

"See," Mary Alice began, "before the twins went away to Columbus—before you came—we started this . . ." She drew a breath. "This *club*. And now," she hurried on, "they're coming over to have a meeting of it."

Patty swallowed hard. Her throat had begun to ache the way it did when Dad went away. A club, without her! It wasn't *fair*. "Well, couldn't I—" She stopped herself. She wasn't going to beg. If Mary Alice didn't want her in it. . . .

"I told them you were here, Patty," Mary Alice said quickly. "As soon as the twins come over, I'm going to ask them about letting you be in it."

"Thanks," Patty mumbled. But what if the twins didn't want her? That would be two against one. And what would she do all day if the three of them went off without her?

"There's Buddy Engle riding your bike!" Mary Alice looked down the street. "Did you say he could?"

"Sort of." Patty watched Buddy pump easily toward them.

"Hi-yo, Silver!" He pulled up at the curb with a squeal of tires. "Hi, Mary Alice. You come over to go riding with Patty?"

"Nope." Mary Alice looked embarrassed. "I better go home," she said quickly. "I'll call you later, Patty." She jumped onto her bike and rode off.

"Want me to put the Imperial away for you?" Buddy patted the handlebars possessively.

"*I* can do it." Patty grabbed the bike away from him and wheeled it toward the house, determined not to drop it. Boy, she thought angrily, kicking its stand down and setting it straight. If I could just ride this thing, I wouldn't even care about their dumb club. Without a backward glance at Buddy, she walked up the steps and went inside.

"Why, Patty!" Grandma looked up and smiled. She was shaping a round of dough between her hands, and a pie pan filled with sliced peaches sat on the table in front of her. "I thought I saw Mary Alice out front with you just now, when I came up to the house."

"She had to go home." Patty didn't want to explain why. It would just make things worse to have Grandma feel sorry for her.

"Mrs. Engle told me the Staley girls had to come back, on account of the polio down to Columbus," Grandma said. "It's just terrible the way that disease jumps around from one place to another." She sighed. "Leastways, it's nice you have your little friends back to play with."

"Yeah." Patty tried to look glad. "Grandma," she asked, "can I roll out the top crust for you?"

"Why, sure." Grandma set the lump of dough down in front of her and went to light the oven.

Patty picked up a soft fistful of flour, rubbed it over the rolling pin and the table, and began to push down at the round of dough the way Grandma had taught her, in short, quick strokes away from the center. The dough started to spread out, soft and elastic, under her rolling pin. Patty lifted the thick circle carefully, turned it over, and pressed down again. There was something comforting about watching the dough thin out beneath her hands. She sprinkled a little flour on top of it.

"Grandma," she said, suddenly remembering. "When are they going to tell who won the flour-naming contest?"

"Most any day now," Grandma said. "Now, don't go getting your heart set on it, Patty, but if I *should* win the prize, I want to give you two dollars of it, to spend for yourself."

"Thanks, Grandma!" With two dollars she could take Mary Alice to Isaly's, and buy something in Woolworth's besides. She wouldn't even ask the twins to come. *Then* they'd be sorry. Patty thumped down hard on the dough.

"Darn it!" A little piece of it stuck to the rolling pin and ripped out of the smooth, flat circle.

Grandma bent to look. "Never mind. We can patch that up so's it won't show at all."

She set the scrap of dough over the torn place and pressed down firmly. "See there? When it's baked, that'll fill right in and you won't even see it."

"Thanks." Patty lifted the stretchy circle of dough from the table and laid it down over the sliced peaches in the pie pan. It fit just right, with enough left over to make a nice rim. She sealed the edges together and pricked a pattern of fork-holes into the top. Even with the patch, the crust looked pretty. But she had wanted it to be perfect. She sighed. *Nothing* was coming out perfect this summer.

"Don't that look nice!" said Grandma approvingly. "We'll bake it right up and have hot peach pie for lunch." She opened the oven door and pushed the pie inside.

There was a sudden knock at the door.

"Now, who could that be?" Grandma straightened up, tugging her apron off, and went to the door.

Patty looked up in surprise. A big man with scraggly gray hair and lines around his eyes stood outside, peering in. He wore baggy pants and a shirt too small for his arms. In one hand he held a suitcase tied together with rope, and in the other he squeezed a shapeless felt hat.

"Mornin', ma'am. Mornin', sis," he said in a soft voice. "How are you folks today?"

Grandma stepped back.

"I'm looking for work," the man said quickly. "Lawn chores, house cleaning, anything." He looked pleadingly at Grandma. "I'm not asking for pay, ma'am. Just for something to eat."

"Well, I don't know." Grandma touched her hair nervously.

Patty stared at the stranger. Where could he have come from? Suddenly, she remembered the funny marks on the Kallmeyers' telephone pole. Could this man be a *spy*?

"I'm an honest man," the stranger said, as though he had read her mind. "Down on my luck, that's all." He paused. In an even softer voice, he said, "I'm hungry."

Patty felt ashamed. She had probably said those very words hundreds of times in her life without ever meaning them. But from the look in the tall man's eyes, she understood that he really did. She looked anxiously at Grandma. Even if he *was* a spy, they had to give him something to eat.

Grandma seemed to have made up her mind. "I've got a screen door needs patching up," she said briskly.

"Maybe you could do that for me."

"Yes, ma'am." The stranger looked so relieved. "Where—"

"Oh, you'll want a bite to eat before you start in," said Grandma, as though this was a friend who had just stopped in to visit. "There's a faucet outside. You can wash up while I fix you a sandwich, Mister—?"

"Swenson," the man said. "John Swenson, traveling man. And I'm much obliged to you for your kindness, ma'am."

"I'll be obliged to you for fixing my door," Grandma said. "But I'll expect to pay you for your work. Is twenty-five cents an hour agreeable to you?"

"Very agreeable." Mr. Swenson smiled. He picked up his suitcase. "Now, if you'll excuse me, I'll go and wash." He started down the back steps.

"I'm glad you had work for him," Patty said. "He looked so hungry, Grandma."

"There's lots of hungry men like him these days." Grandma took a covered dish out of the icebox. "Without work to do or a place to lay their heads." She began to slice into a loaf of bread. "A couple of nice meat-loaf sandwiches, a fresh tomato—that'll taste real good to him. And when the pie's baked up we'll cut him a piece, for a treat. I bet he hasn't tasted home-baked pie in many a day."

"Where do you think he came from?" Patty didn't want to bring up spies, for fear of worrying Grandma.

"From pretty near anywhere." Grandma sliced into the meat loaf. "There's too many places in this country where a man can't find work to support himself, no matter how hard he looks. That's why they take to the road." She glanced out of the window. "It's a shame, a decent man like that. It must be lonesome, wandering all over by himself."

"I know it." Patty wondered what Mary Alice would say about Mr. Swenson. I won't even tell her, she decided resentfully. What does she care about people's feelings? All she cares about is the twins, and their stupid club.

"They say the Lord will provide," Grandma went on. "But the Lord can't do it by himself. He needs human beings to carry out his will, look out for each other in need." She poured milk into a tall glass. "It seems as though hardly a week this summer's gone past without some poor man like Mr. Swenson come knocking on my door."

"Do they go to the Kallmeyers', too?" Patty couldn't imagine Mrs. Kallmeyer being kind to a stranger who might be a spy, or have germs.

"It's a funny thing," said Grandma. "I said to May just the other day, I said, 'You'd think some of those men would find their way next door to the Kallmeyers', instead of every man Jack of them heading straight for this house.'" She laughed. "May said they must spread the word around about my home cooking. I don't know about that, but it does seem I get more than my share of hungry men."

She went out carrying a plate and a glass. Patty heard her talking to Mr. Swenson at the bottom of the steps. "Enjoy your dinner," she called, coming back into the kitchen. She lowered her voice. "A man could make himself sick, choking down a meal on an empty stomach," she told Patty.

"I feel so sorry for him," Patty said. "It doesn't seem fair for some people to have lots to eat and other people not have anything."

"It isn't fair, and that's the truth," Grandma said. "Leastways, we can give thanks we have enough to share." She looked seriously at Patty. "Now, I want you to listen to me, honey. Most of the men who come to this door are good, honest folks who wouldn't hurt a fly. But I want you to promise that if any stranger comes by when May or I aren't here, you won't let him inside." She put her hand on Patty's. "I don't want to worry you, just to be on the safe side. Do you understand?"

"Yes, Grandma." Patty didn't like to think about the dishonest men—maybe real spies—who might come knocking at the door. That was the kind of thing that could stick in your head and give you bad dreams at night.

The telephone rang.

"Hello," Grandma said into the receiver. "Why, isn't that nice!" She smiled at Patty. "Oh, she'll be tickled to see the twins. I'll send her over soon as she washes up."

Patty swallowed.

"Mrs. Kallmeyer wants you to eat lunch with Mary Alice and the twins," Grandma said. "They're over there now. So you wash up quick and scoot over."

"What about Mr. Swenson's pie?" asked Patty, delaying.

"I'll keep an eye on it, don't you worry," said Grandma. "And you can have your piece at supper-time. Go on, now, Patty. You don't want to keep the girls waiting on you."

Reluctantly, Patty went to the sink. She washed her hands slowly and dried them on the roller towel. Then she went to the door and looked down. Mr. Swenson was sitting on the bottom step, with his plate and glass on the step above him.

"Coming down?" He got stiffly to his feet.

"Excuse me." Patty went down the stairs slowly, stepping carefully around the dishes.

"No trouble at all." Mr. Swenson made a little bow, waving her on. "Let me tell you something," he said as she reached the bottom. "Your grandmother's a wonderful cook. It's been many a long day since I ate a dinner good as this."

"There's going to be peach pie for dessert," Patty confided. "I helped to make it."

"Peach pie!" Mr. Swenson beamed. "Well, isn't that something." He winked at Patty. "I bet you're going to be a fine cook, like your grandma."

Patty nodded shyly, pleased.

Mr. Swenson reached out to touch her hair.

"You're a good girl," he said. "I had a little girl about the size of you, once. Long ago, and far away."

Something in his tone kept Patty from asking where

that little girl was now. She wished she could stay here talking to Mr. Swenson, instead of going next door to face the twins.

"Going to have a ride?" Mr. Swenson pointed his thumb at the bicycle.

"No." Patty shook her head. "I'm just going next door, to my friend's house."

"Well, you have a nice time." Mr. Swenson settled himself on the step again.

"Thanks." If he only knew! Patty turned away reluctantly. "Good-bye, Mr. Swenson."

The dry grass crunched under her sandals as she crossed the lawn and made her way slowly around the side of the Kallmeyers' house. When she came to the front, she stopped short and gasped. The twins' bicycles—beautiful blue Elgins with fat white tires—were parked side by side on the Kallmeyers' front walk, like a double image from her vanished dream.

Blinking in the sun, Patty walked by them and stumbled up the Kallmeyers' steps, trying hard not to cry.

SEVEN

Inside, Jeannie was playing the piano. The chords of "Juanita" rippled out through the window: "Neeta, Wa-ah-ah-neeta, Ask thy soul, If we should part . . ." The sad melody fit Patty's mood. She drew a breath and knocked.

The music stopped. Jeannie came to the door in shorts and a halter, a bright streak of orange lipstick across her mouth.

"Hi, Patty." She held the door open. "Come on in. The girls are in the kitchen. I bet you can't wait to see the twins!"

"Yeah." Patty could hardly see in the dark front hall.

"Go on. They're waiting for you." Jeannie waved toward the back of the house.

Patty groped her way through the dim rooms and stopped in the kitchen doorway. Mrs. Kallmeyer's back was turned. Mary Alice and the twins sat at one end of the table, laughing. Patty wondered if they were laughing about her. Had Mary Alice brought up letting her into the club?

The twins looked up at the same moment.

"Hi, Patty," they said together, staring at her.

"Hi." Patty stared back. The twins looked different in some way. Older. It was their hair, she realized suddenly. It was curled in tight, frizzy clumps all over their heads.

Mrs. Kallmeyer pulled out a chair at the other end of the table. "Sit down, Patty dear." She beamed. "Isn't this nice, the four of you together again!"

Patty slid into the chair, bumping her shin against the table leg. She always felt babyish around the twins, even though they were only three months older. They acted like the kids back home—loud and sure of themselves and superior. They knew the words to the latest songs and the stories of all the new movies. They had already heard just about every joke Patty tried to tell, and they always came bursting out with the last lines before she could get to them.

"Did you hear why we had to come back from Columbus?" Myrna asked, looking very important. "There's a big polio epidemic down there."

"And we know a boy who got it," Erna went right on. "First his leg hurt and then he felt sick all over and they took him to the hospital and it turned out he had polio. He might not be able to walk again in his whole *life*."

Or ride a bike! For one shameful second, Patty felt envious of such a perfect excuse.

"I just hate to think of that poor boy's mother," Mrs. Kallmeyer said. "Sick with the worry." She shook her head. "It's a real blessing you girls got away in time, before who knows what might have happened." She set a glass of milk in front of Patty. "How do you like the twins' new hairdos? They got themselves permanents, down to Columbus. Don't they look cute?"

Patty nodded politely, trying not to look at Mary Alice. She was sure that in private, Mary Alice would have laughed at the twins' dumb hairdos. But now that she was in a club with them, she probably wouldn't even smile.

Myrna patted her frizzy curls complacently. "We got them at a beauty parlor."

"The woman who owns it's sister is a friend of Grandma's," Erna added. "So we got them free. Everybody in Columbus has permanents," she said smugly. "You kids ought to get them."

"Not me," Mary Alice said, so firmly that Mrs. Kallmeyer raised a warning eyebrow.

"I mean," Mary Alice explained, "it looks good on you guys, but I don't know if it would on me."

"Your hair's naturally curly anyway," Myrna said. "But Patty—"

"Patty looks good with braids," Mary Alice broke in.

Patty shot her a grateful look. Mary Alice was so loyal! She *must* have asked the twins to let her in the club.

Mrs. Kallmeyer set a plate of egg-salad sandwiches on the table. "Mary Alice, I have to go get ready for my Ladies' Aid meeting, so I'm going to let you be the little hostess for your friends. There's Jell-O in the icebox you can serve up for dessert."

She untied her apron, looking out the window. "Why, Patty, there's a strange-looking man sitting on

61

your Grandma's back steps! Looks as if she gave him some food." She frowned. "Your grandmother's awful trusting. Who knows what terrible germs a person like that might have on him?" Shaking her head, she left the kitchen.

Mary Alice turned to look out. "Maybe he's a spy!" she said eagerly. "We could trail him and see where he goes, the way Orphan Annie did."

"He's not a spy," Patty said. "He's just a regular man. His name's Mr. Swenson. He even has a little girl."

"How do *you* know?" Erna demanded.

"He told me," Patty said defiantly.

The twins exchanged a look.

"He could have been lying," said Myrna. "You can't believe everything people tell you," she added. "Especially if they're spies."

Patty bit into her sandwich without answering. She knew Mr. Swenson wasn't a liar or a spy. He wasn't dirty, either. He'd washed his hands before he'd eaten, like anybody else. She swallowed hard. She wouldn't argue with the twins now, before the subject of the club came up.

"Hey, Patty," said Erna. "Did you see our new bikes?"

Patty swallowed again.

"Aren't they swell?" Myrna looked at her pityingly. "We saw *your* bike when we came over. It's funny-looking."

"It's English." Patty tried to sound casual. "That's the way English bikes are supposed to look. The King

62

of England has one just like it," she added, to impress them.

"Who cares?" Myrna shot back. "This is the U.S.A. I bet the King would rather have an Elgin, anyway. They're the best."

"English bikes are supposed to be good, though," Mary Alice said tactfully. She got up to take a bowl of Jell-O from the icebox, and began spooning it into glass dishes. "Listen, you guys." She looked at the twins. "When do you want to tell Patty about—" She paused. "*You* know."

Patty tried to sound innocent. "About what?"

"About the club," Erna said. "See, before we went away, we started this secret club. The S.P. Club." She smiled at Patty. "And just now, before you came over, we voted to let you be in it."

"Thanks," Patty said, relieved. "What does S.P. stand for?"

"That's a secret," Myrna told her. "Only official club members get to know."

Patty poked a spoon at her Jell-O, trying to guess. Swimming Party? That wouldn't make sense. Silver Pennies, like the name of her poetry book? The twins probably didn't know about that. Suddenly she had an idea. "I bet I know," she burst out eagerly. "Swell People?"

Erna laughed scornfully. "Don't try to guess. After the initiation, we'll tell you."

"What initiation?" Patty looked anxiously at Mary Alice.

"*Your* initiation," said Myrna. "To be in the club,

63

you have to be initiated first. Right?" she asked the others.

"Right." Erna giggled, pushing her Jell-O dish away. "Come on. Let's do it now."

Myrna jumped up. "Patty has to go away, then. So we can get ready."

"Go where?" Patty asked, not liking this.

"Out on the porch or somewhere. It doesn't matter. Just so you can't see," Erna said.

What were they going to do to her?

"It won't take us long." Mary Alice began to clear the table. "Go on, Patty."

"Get out!" Erna gave her a little push.

"I *am*."

Patty walked slowly out of the kitchen, listening to the laughter and whispering behind her, and wondering if the only reason the twins agreed to have her in the club was so they could do something mean to her first.

Jeannie looked up from the piano as Patty walked by. "Going home already?"

"No. I have to wait outside. They're getting ready to initiate me."

Jeannie laughed lightly. "Oh-oh. I guess *you're* in for it."

Patty opened the screen door and sank down onto the glider. Why hadn't Mary Alice said anything about an initiation? It was no fun to wait out here while they were thinking up tricks to play on her. She was almost tempted to duck back home and get out of the whole thing. But only a baby would do that. Besides, she had

64

to be in the club. It would spoil her whole visit if she wasn't. She leaned back against the glider, staring absently through the lilacs.

There was Mr. Swenson! He was walking up the sidewalk with his suitcase in his hand.

Patty sat up straight. I better warn him not to come here, she thought. Mrs. Kallmeyer would probably slam the door in his face.

But Mr. Swenson didn't turn in at the Kallmeyers' walk. Instead, he walked straight toward the telephone pole with the strange marks on it and bent down to look at them. Patty felt a shiver of apprehension. How did he know they were there? Could he be a spy after all?

Mr. Swenson studied the pole for a minute. Then he straightened up, glanced back at the Kallmeyers' house, and walked quickly away in the opposite direction.

Patty sank back in her seat. He hadn't seen her. She peered out through the lilac leaves and watched him disappear around the corner. Her heart was thumping. No matter *what* he is, she told herself, I'm not going to tell on him.

"Close your eyes!" The girls burst through the screen door, giggling. "We're ready!"

EIGHT

"Don't worry," Mary Alice whispered, tying a dish-towel blindfold over Patty's eyes. "It's not going to hurt or anything."

Patty opened her eyes behind the cloth, but all she could see was soft white light. Someone took her hand and led her down the steps.

"Over here!" one of the twins called. "Have you got the stuff?"

"I've got it," said the other one. "Make her sit."

Someone took her arm and pulled her down. She sat awkwardly, feeling foolish behind her blindfold.

Mary Alice began to speak in a loud, unnatural voice. "Okay, Patty. You are now about to be initiated into the S.P. Club of Clearwater, Ohio." She cleared her throat. "The initiation has two parts. In the first part, you must show how brave you are by washing your hands in a basin of blood, and by eating the raw eyeballs—" Her voice broke into a giggle. "The raw eyeballs of a dead dog!"

"Mary Alice!" one of the twins said. "Come on. This is supposed to be serious."

Mary Alice took Patty's hand. "Are you ready?"

Patty could tell she was laughing. She almost laughed back in relief. Blood and eyeballs! She might be a scaredy-cat, but she wasn't dumb enough to believe that. This initiation might not be so bad after all.

"I'm ready," she said.

"Hasten, Jason, bring the basin!" commanded Mary Alice, starting to laugh again.

Someone set a tin bowl in front of Patty's knees.

Mary Alice guided Patty's hands toward it. "Wash!" she directed.

Cautiously, Patty lowered her fingertips into the bowl. "Aaah!" she shouted, drawing back as she touched a thick, slimy liquid. "What *is* this?" Whatever it was, it felt disgusting.

"Human blood!" shrieked a twin. "Go on—rub your hands in it."

Patty dipped her hands into the bowl and rubbed them lightly together. A faint scent of Jell-O reached her nose. So that was what it was! Boldly, she plunged both hands in and rubbed them together vigorously, enjoying the shrieks of horror around her.

"Oooh, Patty, how can you!"

"Human *blood*!"

Patty wiped her sticky hands on the grass. "Where are the eyeballs?" she asked, beginning to enjoy this. It was sort of nice to be the center of attention.

"Hold out your hand," said a twin.

"Eeeh!" In spite of herself, Patty drew back as two gooey blobs fell onto her palm. What were they? She knew they couldn't be eyeballs, but they felt the way eyeballs would. She shuddered.

The girls laughed.

"Eat them!" said Mary Alice.

Patty hesitated a minute before she tossed the blobs into her open mouth. She gagged as they touched her tongue, but then the sweet taste of grape juice came through.

"Grapes!" she shouted triumphantly, swallowing them. "Now can I take off the blindfold?"

"Let her," said a twin, sounding disappointed. "I *told* you guys those things weren't going to fool her."

Patty tugged off her blindfold, blinking at the bright sunlight. The others were sitting in a circle around her, grinning. "They were good, though," she said generously, looking down at her red hands. "What was that stuff in the basin, anyway?"

"Jell-O and ketchup!" said Erna.

"Well, it felt pretty much like blood." Patty had a sudden wonderful sense of belonging. Now she was practically in the club! "What do I have to do next?" she asked.

Myrna jumped up, laughing. "You'll see. Come on, you guys. Let's go over there." She pointed to a grassy slope by the Kallmeyers' unmowed side lot. "You kids sit on the hill and watch, and I'll do it."

"Do what?" Patty asked, as Myrna pulled her down the slope and into the rough grass.

"Wait." Myrna turned around. "Sit down, you two," she called. "Okay, Patty," she said solemnly. "This is the last part of your initiation into the S.P.

Club. If we let you in, do you promise faithfully to keep all club secrets and abide by all club rules?"

Patty nodded.

"*What* rules?" Mary Alice called. "I didn't know we had any."

"Well, as soon as we get some, she has to obey them," Myrna said. "Now, listen, Patty. You probably didn't know this, but the S.P. Club is connected to the country of Siam."

"Siam?" Patty asked suspiciously as the audience giggled.

"In Siam they have a secret chant that everyone knows," Myrna went on. "And now you have to learn it, too." She raised her hand and stared at Patty solemnly. "Raise your hand and repeat these words after me: Oh, wa—"

Patty put her hand up. "Oh, wa."

"Ta, goo," Myrna went on.

"Ta, goo."

"Siam!" Myrna finished, laughing.

"Siam!" Patty wondered what was funny.

"Very good," Myrna said. "Now you must say it the official way. Watch." She squatted down and put her hands under her arms, raising and lowering her elbows. "Get down."

Patty squatted low and copied Myrna's movements awkwardly. "Like this?"

Myrna straightened up. "Yeah. But now you have to start jumping and moving your arms while you say the words."

How could she jump in this dumb position?

Patty looked helplessly at Erna and Mary Alice.

"Go on, Patty," Erna called. "Move!"

Patty took a little jump, wiggling her arms up and down. "Oh, wa," she said softly.

"Louder!" Myrna said. "Jump faster."

Patty jumped again. "Oh, wa. Ta, goo." She lost her balance, then steadied herself. "Siam!" She pumped her elbows up and down, moving over the rough grass. "Can I stop now?" Her legs were aching, and sweat was breaking out on her upper lip.

On the bank, Erna and Mary Alice were screaming with laughter.

"Again!" Myrna said.

Doggedly, Patty jumped forward in her awkward crouch, moving her arms up and down. The grass scratched her legs. She felt ridiculous, but she'd show them she could do it. She wasn't going to give up now. "Oh, wa, ta, goo, Siam!" she gasped. "Oh, wa, ta, goo, Siam. *OhwatagooSiam!*"

Suddenly, she realized what she was saying. She scrambled angrily to her feet as the girls ran up to her, howling.

"What a goose she is!"

"She said so herself!"

Patty brushed the grass from her shorts, trying to regain her lost dignity. "Boy. Of all the dumb tricks!"

"Mary *Alice!*" Jeannie called from the porch. "What are you kids doing in the side lot? Don't you know there's poison ivy out there?"

Mary Alice gave a guilty gasp. "Oh-oh," she said. "Come on, you guys." She started toward the house.

"It's okay," she called to Jeannie. "We aren't playing there anymore."

"*Is* there poison ivy in there?" Myrna asked. "I sure hope I didn't get it."

"Well, what about *me*?" Patty demanded.

"Don't worry," Mary Alice said easily. "You were only in there a couple of minutes."

"What a goose you were!" Erna was still laughing. "You should have seen yourself, Patty!"

"Well, Myrna was a goose, too," Patty retorted, suddenly feeling proud of herself. After all, she'd made it through the whole initiation. And now . . .

Mary Alice smiled at her. "Now you're in the club."

"Who wants to be?" Patty shot back. "If all you do is play dumb tricks on people." It was sort of nice to hear herself talking in this kidding way, like the kids back home. Maybe getting through the initiation had given her confidence.

"It was just a joke." Myrna put her arm around Patty's waist and pulled her on.

"Well, it wasn't funny." Patty couldn't help smiling. Now that it was over, she had to admit that the Siam trick was pretty good. Maybe she could play it on somebody else sometime. "Hey," she said, hopping a little to get in step with Myrna. "Now you have to tell me what S.P. stands for."

Myrna put her mouth to Patty's ear. "The Special Pals Club!"

Patty wiped away the spit. "What's so great about that? Anybody could have thought of it."

"You didn't," Erna pointed out in a friendly way.

She walked backwards, facing them. "What do you guys want to do now?"

"Does the club do secret stuff?" asked Patty hopefully.

The girls looked at each other.

"Not that much," Myrna admitted. "We just do regular things, like ride bikes and stuff."

"Hey, let's go ride now!" suggested Erna.

Patty's heart sank. She glanced at Mary Alice. "I can't," she made herself say. "I don't know how to ride yet."

Myrna looked surprised. "How come your aunt got you that bike, then?"

"So I could learn on it. Only, so far I didn't."

Mary Alice turned to the twins. "Why don't you let Patty try riding one of your bikes? They'd be a lot easier to learn on."

"I don't know—" Patty hesitated.

"Mom would kill us if anything happened to our bikes," Myrna said after a pause.

"Nothing would happen," Mary Alice insisted. "Come on."

"Well—okay," said Myrna. "She can take mine. But be careful with it, Patty." She went to her bike and wheeled it over. "Here."

Patty took the handlebars, looking down at the bright blue fenders and the solid white tires. It would be so wonderful just to climb on and ride! If she could—

Mary Alice grabbed the seat. "Get on, Patty. I'll hold you."

Patty straddled the frame, raising herself up until she felt the seat beneath her. The bike wobbled when she set her weight down, but Mary Alice held it straight. Slowly, Patty put one foot on the pedal.

"Put the other one on," said Mary Alice.

Patty raised her other foot and put it down. The bike stood firm.

"Pedal!" said Mary Alice.

"Come on, Myrna," Erna said. "I'll ride you on my bike while Patty has yours."

Myrna jumped onto the seat and Erna pushed them off, guiding the bicycle down the walk and out into the street. Patty watched enviously as they swooped away. Myrna stuck her legs out stiffly, holding on, while Erna pumped down hard on one side and then the other. They made it look so easy!

"See? All you need is a little practice." Mary Alice adjusted her grip. "Come on, Patty. Pedal. I'm going to start pushing."

"Don't let go!" Patty yelled.

"I won't." Mary Alice gave her a shove. "Pedal!"

"Wait a sec." Patty arranged her feet, grabbing the hand grips as tightly as she could.

"Here you go!" Mary Alice pushed harder. The bike began to roll.

Patty pushed down on one pedal, and then the other as the bike jerked ahead. "I'm doing it!" she yelled. "Mary Alice, keep holding!" The bike was bouncing across the lawn.

"Hey, slow up! Wait for me!" Suddenly, Mary Alice let go. "Wait!" she shouted. "Brake, Patty!"

The bike rolled ahead, gathering speed. Patty tried to stop it, but her foot slipped off the pedal. The wheel turned sharply and the bicycle tilted to the right.

"Help!" Patty yelled, as the ground came rushing toward her. "Catch me! I can't stop!"

For a breathless instant the bike swayed in place. Then it fell to the ground, carrying Patty with it.

"Patty!" Mary Alice ran up. "Are you okay?"

"I guess so." Shaking, Patty grabbed Mary Alice's arm and pulled herself up. Her leg stung from the scrape, and sharp twinges ran up and down her elbow, making her stomach throb. "Oh, Mary Alice," she blurted out as Erna came pumping furiously toward them. "When am I *ever* going to learn?"

"What happened?" Erna pulled up sharply and both twins jumped off.

"I thought you said you'd be careful," said Myrna, lifting her bicycle up and brushing grass from its fender. "Boy, Patty, if you hurt this bike, I'm really going to be mad at you."

"She didn't—" Mary Alice began.

Patty blinked back the tears. "I didn't mean to fall," she said angrily. "Anyway, what kind of Special Pals are you, if all you care about is your dumb bikes?"

"You're just jealous," Myrna shot back. "Just because you don't have an Elgin—"

"I don't *want* an Elgin!" Patty shouted furiously. "I don't want to be in your dumb club, either," she rushed on, unable to stop herself. "I quit!" She brushed the hair out of her eyes, confronting the twins. "I wish you'd stayed in Columbus," she burst out. She drew a breath. "I wish you'd caught *polio!*"

"*Patty!*" cried Mary Alice.

The twins stared at her in astonishment.

For a second, Patty stared back defiantly. Then, with her words still ringing in her ears, she turned away abruptly and stumbled back across the lawn to Grandma's.

NINE

Patty's heart thumped furiously in her chest as she tugged at the screen door and let herself onto the porch. Little sun spots swam in front of her eyes. Breathing hard, she steadied herself against the door frame and twisted around to look at the back of her leg. The scraped place had turned a bright pink. Carefully, Patty adjusted her shorts so it wouldn't show. Then she wiped her eyes on her sleeve and stepped into the house. How would she explain to Grandma why she had come back so soon?

But Grandma didn't ask. She came bursting in from the kitchen, waving a letter and smiling with excitement.

"What do you think's happened?" She pulled Patty to her. "Your grandma's won her contest, that's what! They're going to call it Golden Crust Flour!"

"Oh, boy!" For a minute, Patty forgot the fight. "That's swell, Grandma!"

"Just listen to this." Grandma began to read aloud. " 'Dear Mrs. Schultz: Congratulations! The Ohio Milling Company has selected your entry—Golden Crust

Flour—as the winning name in the contest to name our new product. In appreciation, we are sending you five bags of Golden Crust Flour.'"

Grandma beamed at Patty over her glasses. "Land, won't it be wonderful to see my own name on all those bags!" she said. "'And we enclose our check in the sum of twenty-five dollars.'" She studied the words and said them again. "*Twenty-five dollars!* What do you think of that? Just wait till your Aunt May hears about it. My, but she's going to be tickled. And I can't wait to see Alma Engle's face when she hears."

"I know." Patty wished that *she* could run out and tell somebody. It would be so wonderful to impress Mary Alice and the twins.

"I'll just run down to Alma's now." Grandma took her pocketbook from the coat rack and stuffed the envelope into it. "Take my check along to show her." She reached for her hat. "And I might as well go right on down to the bank afterwards and cash it." She smiled at Patty. "Don't forget. Grandma promised to give you two dollars for your own if she won the contest, and that's just what she's going to do." She paused in the doorway to push her hat pin in. "Isn't it nice that the Staley girls are back? Now you can take them and Mary Alice all out for a treat somewhere."

Patty tried to smile. "Thanks a lot, Grandma."

"I won't be gone long," Grandma said. "If May comes home, go ahead and tell her the news." Clasping her pocketbook tightly beneath her arm, she went out.

For a minute, Patty stood at the door and watched

Grandma hurry down the sidewalk. Then, with a sob, she threw herself face down on the couch and buried her face in a pillow, letting the tears run out.

"Why, Patty!" Aunt May burst through the door carrying her golf clubs. "Whatever's the matter?"

Patty pulled herself up, not even trying to hide her tears. "Grandma won the contest! They're going to name the flour Golden Crust, and they sent her twenty-five dollars!"

"Why, that's wonderful!" Aunt May sat down beside Patty and stroked her hair gently. "That's nothing to cry about, hon."

"I know!" Patty sobbed out. "Only—" She looked helplessly at her aunt. "Everything's so awful!" she burst out. "I fell off Myrna's bike, and I quit the club we were in, and all the kids are mad at me." She tried to catch her breath. "And Grandma's giving me two whole dollars, and I can't even tell anybody." She might as well say it all. "And I want to ride my bike so bad, but I'm scared!" She pressed her face against Aunt May's shoulder.

"Well, goodness," said Aunt May. "Sounds like you've got quite a lot to cry about." She reached into her pocket for a handkerchief and wiped Patty's face. "Now, then," she said, "that *is* good news about Grandma, isn't it?"

"Oh, yes." Patty sat up, trying to smile. "It's swell! If only—"

"I'll bet the girls would love to hear about it," Aunt May went on. "Why don't you go wash your face, and just run right over and tell them?"

"I *can't!*" In her mind, Patty saw the girls' shocked faces. "They're too mad at me."

"Even Mary Alice?" Aunt May asked gently. "I can't imagine Mary Alice staying mad at you." She smiled. "I remember when the two of you were little girls, you were always getting into terrible arguments, but you could never manage to stay angry very long. You'd come running home crying, and ten minutes later Mary Alice would be over here wanting to know if you could play."

"This is different." They weren't little girls anymore.

"Not that different," said Aunt May. "All you have to do is go over and say you're sorry, and then—"

"I *can't!*" Patty said again. "I would if I could, but—"

Aunt May didn't try to argue. "Well, then," she said briskly. "What do you say the two of us go out and have ourselves a bike-riding lesson?"

"Now?" Patty's stomach tightened up. The scrape on her leg began stinging again.

"Why not?" Aunt May asked, smiling. "You know something? I have a feeling you're awfully close to learning how right now."

"You do?" Patty wished she could believe it. "I want to so *much*, but—"

"And that's why you're going to do it," Aunt May said firmly. "You know, everybody's scared of riding at first. I certainly was."

"You were?" Patty was surprised. Aunt May always seemed to do things so easily.

"Oh, yes." Aunt May sat back on the couch. "I still remember the summer I learned. It was when your mother got her bicycle. Oh, how badly I wanted to ride it! But your grandma thought I was too young." She smiled at the memory. "So I had to sneak out, to practice on Jean's bike. It was a secondhand one," she said, "with a very shaky frame that wobbled when you sat on it." She looked ruefully at Patty. "I guess that's why I wanted you to have the Imperial," she explained. "I know it's pretty big for you now. But they told me at the bike shop that it's the strongest, most solid bike made. And the fastest!" she added. "Anyway, I had the hardest time getting the hang of riding. I must have fallen off your Mom's bike dozens of times. And I could never tell your grandma, because I knew she'd scold me."

"Did Mom know?" asked Patty, fascinated.

"Oh, sure. She helped to teach me," said Aunt May. "We used to take the bike down to the park to practice. How I hated falling off in front of the other children there!" She smiled. "And then one day it just seemed to happen. Jean gave me a little push, and I hung on, and all of a sudden I was riding. It was wonderful!" She laughed. "A couple of months after that, I took your Aunt Flo down to the park and taught *her*. All three of us learned on that same rickety old bike."

"Where is it now?" Patty asked.

"Goodness, I don't know what ever happened to that bicycle," Aunt May said thoughtfully. "It's probably on a junk heap somewhere. But *that* won't happen to your Imperial. It's going to last you a good long time." She stood up and held out her hand. "Someday, most bikes will probably be thin and streamlined like yours. And you can always say that you learned to ride on one of the first of them. Come on. Let's go give it a try." .

"Okay." Patty took Aunt May's hand and followed her outside. Wouldn't it be funny, she thought, if other kids started getting streamlined bikes, and I already had one? She pictured herself circling casually around the playground at school, while people begged her for turns.

Aunt May wheeled the bike over. "Climb on, hon."

Patty pulled herself onto the seat, trying not to notice the way it rubbed against her scrape. She held the handlebars tightly, looking down at the gravelly driveway.

"Don't look down," said Aunt May. "Keep your eyes ahead, the way you'll do when you're riding."

Patty raised her eyes, and saw Buddy Engle coming out of his house. For Pete's sake! she thought, shifting uncomfortably on the seat. Why does *he* always have to come around?

Buddy walked up to them, grinning. "Hi, Miss Schultz. Hi, Patty. Having a bike lesson?"

"Yeah." What did he think she was doing—learning to swim?

"Mrs. Schultz just told us she won the contest," Buddy said. "Boy, that's really something. Twenty-five dollars!" He whistled.

81

"Isn't it great?" Aunt May said, letting the bike tip a little as she turned to him.

Patty clung on, hating to be caught just sitting there in front of Buddy.

"I guess everybody in Clearwater's going to be buying Golden Crust Flour," Buddy went on. "That's a real good name."

Was he going to stand here all day? Patty wriggled impatiently on the seat.

"Well, I better get along," Buddy said finally. "Got to go to the hardware store." He stroked the front fender. "Want to give me a ride to town, Patty?"

"Nope," Patty said, annoyed, as he walked away.

"We'll see you, Buddy," Aunt May called. "Now, then, Patty. I think you ought to practice braking first. Once you know you can stop yourself, you'll feel a lot safer." She put her arm around Patty's waist. "Try it. Push the pedals around and then back them up a little till you feel the brakes catch."

Carefully, Patty pushed down and back. The bike jerked.

"Steady!" said Aunt May. "Do you see how it feels? Keep trying that awhile. Pedal, stop, pedal, stop, pedal, stop—that's it!"

"Hey, I see how you do it," Patty said, pleased. "It really stops fast."

"Oh, the Imperial has wonderful brakes." Aunt May moved to the back of the bike, still holding on. "Now I'm going to push you forward, and you brake." She shoved the bike gently ahead. "Pedal. Keep pedaling. Now, brake!"

Patty pressed back and the bike stopped. She felt for the ground with the toes of one foot and looked around at Aunt May.

"See? You did it," said Aunt May. "Now this time I'm going to push you on out into the street."

"Don't push too fast!" Patty cried.

"I won't." Aunt May gave a gentle shove. The bike began to roll. "Start pedaling."

"Don't let go!" Patty held on tightly, trying to keep her eyes straight ahead.

"I'm right here," Aunt May said calmly, behind her. "Get set to stop if you have to." Half-running behind the bike, she began to push faster. "Here we go!"

The bike bounced into the street. Patty guided the wheel into a turn, pumping harder as it rolled ahead. Pedaling fast like this seemed to hold the bike steady. She glanced down at the street beneath her feet.

"Look up!" Aunt May shouted.

Patty raised her eyes. They were almost halfway down the block!

"Now, brake!" shouted Aunt May.

Patty pressed the pedals back hard. The bike stopped short, tipping to the right. "Help!" she yelled, setting her foot down.

"You're all right," said Aunt May. "I've got you. You were really doing well, Patty. Just remember not to brake too suddenly." She guided the bike into a turn. "Let's see you pump even faster on the way back. Ready?" Holding on, she gave the bicycle a strong push. "Good!" she called, running behind Patty. "Faster!"

Patty pedaled as hard as she could, feeling the bike roll ahead steadily. Her braids thumped against the back of her neck.

"Turn," Aunt May directed, as they neared the driveway. "Pedal right on up."

Patty turned the wheel smoothly and guided the bicycle up the driveway, braking as gently as she could when she reached the steps. Then she put one foot onto the ground and slid off, grinning triumphantly at Aunt May.

"That was wonderful!" Aunt May said. "You were practically riding by yourself, do you know that? You were going so fast I could hardly hold on."

Patty nodded, out of breath, sneaking a glance over at the Kallmeyers'. If only Mary Alice and the twins had been watching!

But they couldn't have been, for at that very moment the Kallmeyers' front door slammed and they all ran out of the house, shouting. The twins climbed onto their bikes and circled the yard while Mary Alice went behind the house and came back out front with hers. Then, as Patty watched wistfully, the three of them swooped into the street and rode away together.

❋
TEN

Patty woke suddenly as a streak of sunlight hit her eyes. She sat up, staring blankly at the wallpaper roses while her mind came slowly awake.

Then she remembered. She had no one to play with. They were all mad at her—even Mary Alice. She looked out the window at Mary Alice's drawn shades. If only she could run over and tell her about the contest!

Resolutely, she jumped out of bed and began to get dressed. She'd show them. She'd spend the whole day practicing on her bike. Maybe by tonight, she'd be able to ride right past them.

She ran downstairs and found Grandma and Aunt May in the kitchen.

"Aunt May," she said, sliding into her chair. "Can we go out after breakfast and practice riding some more?"

"Oh, hon, I'm sorry." Aunt May frowned. "I have to spend this whole day up at school. There's a meeting about next year's schedules." She touched Patty's hand. "I guess you'll have to wait until after supper.

Unless you want to practice by yourself. Or ask Mary Alice to help you," she added casually.

"Oh, May, I don't want her doing that," Grandma protested. "She shouldn't get on that bicycle without you. I didn't know you had a meeting today, May," she said anxiously. "Here I went and told Irene Perkins I'd go out to the Old Folks' Home with her. But I hate to leave Patty alone. . . ."

"I'll be all right, Grandma," Patty said quickly, although she hated the thought of spending the day by herself.

"Well, you could run right next door to Kallmeyers', if you needed anything," Grandma said innocently. "Now, Patty, just so's I can leave with an easy mind, promise me you won't let a stranger into the house while I'm gone."

"I won't."

"And you won't light a match to the stove," Grandma went on.

"Mama!" Aunt May broke in. "The next thing, you'll tell her not to stuff beans up her nose."

Patty laughed, remembering Grandma's story about the mother who said that to her children and made them so curious that the minute she had left the house, they did it.

"Won't Irene Perkins be pleased to hear about the contest!" Aunt May said, as though she wanted to take Grandma's mind off possible disasters.

"Land, yes, and all the old folks, too." Grandma beamed. "I still don't hardly believe it myself.

Twenty-five dollars! May, I want you to look around for a nice dress for yourself—"

A car honked in the street. "There's my ride." Hastily, Aunt May gathered her things. "Have a nice day, Mama. You, too, Patty." She ran out.

"My, I hope Irene don't come for me yet," said Grandma, clearing the table. "I'm not half ready."

"Go on and get dressed, Grandma," Patty said. "I'll do the dishes."

"Well, that'd be nice." Grandma peered into the icebox. "There's bologna for your lunch, and cheese, and some tomatoes. There's plenty for Mary Alice, if she wants to eat over here with you. And the twins, too." She pulled off her apron. "If Mrs. Perkins comes, tell her I'll be right there."

"I will."

Patty spooned up her cereal slowly. At lunchtime, she'd have to eat alone. She sighed. It had been so much fun yesterday, after the initiation. Before the fight. The twins could really act nice when they felt like it. Now they probably weren't *ever* going to feel like it. Patty finished her cereal and sipped at the grapefruit juice Grandma had put at her place. It tasted just the way she felt.

Grandma came bustling back into the kitchen in her Sunday dress—navy blue with white polka dots. "Mary Alice ought to be up soon. Then you'll have company." Grandma looked out the window. "Oh my, there's Irene now." She kissed Patty hastily. "Have a nice time!" she called as she went out the door.

Patty watched Grandma get into the car and drive away. She was probably telling Mrs. Perkins all about the contest. If only *she* had someone to tell!

She cleared the table and filled the dishpan with soapy water. She lingered over the dishes, washing them carefully, drying each one and putting everything away.

When she was finished, she looked around. The house seemed awfully quiet. Patty went into the living room and turned on the radio. A ukulele was strumming "Juanita," the theme song of Grandma's favorite morning serial, *The Romance of Helen Trent.* Patty snapped the radio off. Helen Trent was boring. She never did anything except fall in love. Mary Alice said it took Helen Trent from Monday to Friday just to walk across a room. She always made fun of the program. "Tune in tomorrow," she would say in an announcer's deep voice, "to see if Helen Trent gets up out of her chair or not."

Someone knocked on the back door.

Could that be Mary Alice? Patty ran out to open it. Then she stepped back.

It was Mr. Swenson! He held his hat in his hands, smiling hesitantly.

"Hello there, girlie. Your Grandma home?"

"No." Patty felt a shiver of fear.

"That's too bad." Mr. Swenson took a handkerchief from his pocket and wiped his perspiring face. "I was hoping she might have more work for me to do."

"She went out to the Old Folks' Home." As soon as

she said it, Patty wished she hadn't. "She'll be back soon, though," she added quickly.

"That's too bad." Mr. Swenson twisted his hat in his hands. "Fact is, I was kind of hoping she'd give me a bite to eat."

Patty stared at his wrinkled face, trying to forget how she'd seen him last—studying the Kallmeyers' telephone pole like a spy. It was scary to have him suddenly appear like this. Maybe he'd come back to spy on her, or to steal Grandma's prize money!

"I'm not supposed to light the stove," she said, stalling. But the pleading look in his eyes overcame her. He was *hungry*. She drew a quick breath. "I could make you a bologna sandwich, I guess," she said nervously.

Mr. Swenson smiled. "A bologna sandwich would hit the spot," he said. "That's real kind of you."

Patty gave him a towel and a bar of soap. "Would you like to wash up while I fix it?" she asked. At least that would get him off the back porch.

"Thanks a million." Mr. Swenson took the towel and started down the steps.

It was too late to change her mind now. Feeling scared and grown-up all at once, Patty cut four thick slices of bread, spread them with mayonnaise, and covered them with bologna and cheese. She put the sandwiches together, cut them into triangle halves the way Grandma always did, and set them on a plate.

They looked delicious. In spite of the breakfast she'd eaten, Patty felt hungry. She cut two more slices of bread and made another sandwich for herself. She'd eat it in here while Mr. Swenson had his outside.

She chose the ripest tomato, set it on the plate beside the sandwiches, and went to the door. Mr. Swenson had unbuttoned his collar and tied a handkerchief around his neck. He looked up at her, smiling.

"Could I trouble you to bring me down a glass," he asked, "so's I can get myself a drink of water? This heat makes a person real thirsty."

Patty felt the hot sun beating down on her back. The whole yard was sunny, without a spot of shade anywhere. Mr. Swenson could faint from the heat out here, while she sat inside in the cool kitchen. It wasn't fair.

"Would you like to come in to eat?" she asked, shocked at herself. What would Grandma say? Still, whatever else he might be, Mr. Swenson wasn't a stranger.

"Well, now. That would be a pleasure." Holding onto the rail, Mr. Swenson climbed slowly toward her.

Patty held her breath. "Come in," she said formally, when he reached the top. She held the door for him. "Please sit down."

"I thank you." Mr. Swenson stood behind his chair until Patty sat down on hers. Then he sat down, too, with his hands in his lap, and looked gravely at her.

Quickly, Patty folded her hands in front of her and bowed her head. "For what we are about to receive," she said, as Grandma always did, "Dear Lord, we thank thee."

"Amen," Mr. Swenson said softly. Then he raised his head and smiled. "Well," he said. He picked up a sandwich and began to eat, chewing each bite slowly. When he had eaten the first half, he paused. "I guess you're wondering how come I turned up again," he said. "Like a bad penny," he added apologetically.

"Oh, no," Patty said quickly. It was just what she had been wondering.

"I expected to be clear to Missoura by this time." Mr. Swenson leaned forward. "Hopped onto a freight train headed that way right after I saw you last. But the cops caught up with me somewhere in Indiany."

The cops! Patty tried not to show her shock. Was she sitting here alone with a *criminal*? She should have listened to Mary Alice. She swallowed hard. What would Orphan Annie do at a time like this? She'd probably try to get a confession out of him.

Patty leaned forward. "*Why* were the cops after you?" she asked craftily.

Mr. Swenson didn't look the least bit guilty. "Oh, the usual," he said. "Those railway police don't like to see a fella riding free." He smiled wryly. "That's a crime, in their eyes."

"*That's* not—" Patty felt a surge of relief.

"The way I see it," Mr. Swenson told her, "it's a crime when a man who's not looking for anything but an honest day's work has to roam this country trying to find it."

"That's what *I* think!" Patty spoke fervently to cover her embarrassment. How could she have suspected a kind man like him of being a criminal, even for a minute? But still—what about the telephone pole? He had *some* kind of secret.

Mr. Swenson went on with his story. "Anyways, I hid out by the tracks for a while, and when a train came by in the night, headed East, I jumped right onto it. Thought I'd go back to Clearwater, Ohio, look up that lady on Elm Street who cooks so fine, see that pretty little girl again. . . ."

Patty blushed with pleasure. "It must be quite exciting to ride so many trains," she said in her best company tone.

"It is that." Mr. Swenson held up his tomato, looking at it appreciatively. "Now there's a tomato. Ripe as you could ask for." He took a large bite. "Yes," he said thoughtfully, "there's many a hobo who wouldn't ask for anything better than a long, slow ride in a boxcar, with the wheels clanking under him and a hole in the roof big enough to watch the stars through." He stopped to finish the tomato. "As for me," he went on, wiping his mouth, "my old bones can't take the traveling life much longer." He sat back in his chair, a dreamy look in his eyes. "If I had my wish, I'd find me a half-acre somewhere out in the Ozark mountains, with a stream running by and the fish jumping right out of it into my skillet." His voice grew soft. "Build a tight little cabin, get me a coon dog for company. . . ."

"What about your family?" Patty asked him. "Your little girl?"

Mr. Swenson sighed. "My family's long gone," he

said. "I'm all by my lonesome these days." Then he smiled. "Except when I meet up with a sweet little lady like you."

Patty ducked her head shyly. "I sure hope you get your wish, Mr. Swenson." She jumped up and went to the cookie jar. "Would you like a date bar? Grandma made them." She piled some cookies onto a plate and set it in front of him.

"Your Grandma's a wonderful cook." Mr. Swenson bit into a date bar. "Just like they all say."

"*Who* says?" Patty leaned forward.

"Oh, we traveling men have our ways of passing the word along." Mr. Swenson smiled mysteriously. "Where to look for work, which lady's liable to slam a door in your face, which one's a good cook. Don't tell me you never saw a hobo message?"

"I don't think so." Patty was surprised.

Mr. Swenson smiled. "Next time you go out, you take a look at that telephone pole out front of the house next door. You'll be staring right at one."

"Is that what those little marks are?" Patty was excited. That explained everything! If only she could tell Mary Alice!

"Yep. Every one of those chalk marks, that's a message from a man who went before."

"How do you know what they mean?" This was better than any Orphan Annie code!

"Give me a pencil and I'll show you." Mr. Swenson pushed his plate away and took a scrap of paper from his pocket. "Now this here—" He took the pencil and drew a circle with a line sticking out from one side. "This means, 'turn right.' And this—" He drew another circle, with a line coming out the opposite side, and looked up, waiting for Patty to say it.

"Means 'turn left'!" Patty shouted.

"You got it." Mr. Swenson was drawing an up-and-down arrow. "This one means 'straight ahead.' And *this*—" He drew a horizontal line with a lot of short lines hanging from it. "Can you guess?"

Patty stared at it. "I give up."

"Well, that's a picture of a comb. A comb has teeth, and so does—?"

"A dog!" Patty laughed.

Next, Mr. Swenson drew a small circle on top of a big one, with two little checks beside them. "This here one is what brought me to you," he said. "The circles mean 'a kind lady' and the checks say 'She cooks good.'" Mr. Swenson smiled at her. "That's why your grandma gets so many callers. But if you look sharp, you'll see this one out there, too, with an arrow pointing a different direction." He drew a little stick figure with running legs. "That's the one to watch out for. It means 'Run like h—'" He stopped abruptly and cleared his throat. "It means 'Run away fast.'"

"Boy!" Patty grinned. That must be the sign for Mrs. Kallmeyer. She could never tell Mary Alice *that*.

"And now you know the official code of the road." Mr. Swenson handed her the piece of paper. "Well," he said, pushing himself heavily to his feet. "It's time to be getting along, I guess. I thank you for that fine dinner," he said. "*And* for the company. It's not often I sit down at a table and talk with a nice little girl." He pulled one of Patty's braids gently. "Not in many a year."

"Where will you go now?" Patty asked, feeling sorry for him.

"Maybe I'll head across town, find some work to do nearby to the station," Mr. Swenson said. "And then, when that evening train comes through, it'll be westward, ho, for me." He smiled wryly. "Only this time, I'm going to cover myself up good, keep an eye out for those cops."

"Wait," Patty said. "I'll pack you a snack to take along." She wrapped some date bars in waxed paper and put them in a paper sack with an apple and a tomato. "Here." She handed it to Mr. Swenson.

He touched her shoulder gently. "God bless you, girlie." He walked to the door and stood there for a moment, looking at her. Then he went out.

Patty followed him onto the hot back porch. "Goodbye," she said as he picked up his suitcase and started down the steps. "Good-bye, Mr. Swenson!"

At the bottom, Mr. Swenson turned to wave. Then he walked slowly away, without looking back.

Patty stood watching him, with the sun beating down on her back. She wondered if he would ever make it safely all the way to Missouri, and his own little cabin by the mountain stream. If only, she breathed to herself, crossing her fingers for him as he disappeared around the corner.

Just then, Mary Alice came out of her house. "Hey, Patty!" She crossed the lawn and came to the steps, looking up hesitantly.

Patty was still dazed by Mr. Swenson's visit. "Hi, Mary Alice," she said, almost forgetting they were supposed to be mad at each other. It didn't seem that important anymore. Anyway, Mary Alice was smiling.

"Hey, guess what, Mary Alice?" Patty didn't know where to begin. "Guess what?" She jumped down the stairs to stand beside her. "You know those funny little chalk marks on your telephone pole, the ones you said might be spy codes?"

Mary Alice nodded. "What about them?" she asked eagerly.

"Wait till I show you! It *is* a secret code!" Patty put her arm around her friend and pulled her across the grass, hardly bothering to notice how easy making up had been.

❋
ELEVEN

It would be harder to make up with the twins, Patty thought sitting happily on the Kallmeyers' steps with Mary Alice. She wasn't even sure she wanted to.

"You *have* to, Patty," Mary Alice said. "If you don't, what am I supposed to do when they come over? Play with them and not you, or you and not them? That's dumb, when we could all have fun doing stuff together. That's why I wanted you to be in the club in the first place."

"I knew it!" Patty turned on her. "I knew you had to *make* them let me in, Mary Alice. I bet they didn't really want me."

"Yes, they did," said Mary Alice. "Honestly, Patty. They like you. They just don't know you as well as I do." She looked thoughtful. "You know why I think they act kind of mean sometimes? I think they're jealous, because they know you're my best friend."

"Yeah." Patty was pleased that Mary Alice understood.

"Anyway," Mary Alice went on, "after you went home yesterday they said they were sorry."

"Well, they should be," Patty said.

"You ought to be sorry, too, Patty," Mary Alice persisted. "It wasn't the *twins'* fault you fell off Myrna's bike. You didn't have to get so mad at them." She looked seriously at Patty. "That was awful, what you said about polio."

"I know it." If only she hadn't said that! It *was* awful. "I didn't mean it," Patty added weakly. "It was just—the twins act so great, just because they have Elgins. Other bikes are good, too. Imperials are the best in the world. Aunt May said so." She grabbed Mary Alice's shoulder, remembering. "Hey, guess what? I was practically riding last night! Aunt May hardly held on. You should have seen me!" She stopped. Mary Alice *would* have seen her, if she hadn't gone off with the twins.

"That's swell!" said Mary Alice. "What did I tell you? I knew you'd catch on." She pushed a little stone off the step. "Boy," she said, suddenly glum. "Everybody's going to be riding new bikes except me."

"I'm not really riding yet," Patty said quickly, feeling sorry for her. Mary Alice had wanted a new bike for years. But one of Mrs. Kallmeyer's principles was "Waste not, want not." That meant not wasting what she always called good money on a new bike for Mary Alice as long as Jeannie's old one would still go.

"You can use my bike anytime," Patty told her. "You ought to try it, Mary Alice. I bet you could beat anybody with it, it's so fast and streamlined."

"What does that mean?"

"It means thin and fast, not fat and heavy like an

98

Elgin." Patty stood up. "Want to go over and take a ride on it now?"

"No." Mary Alice pulled her down again. "The twins are coming, remember? And you have to apologize. Then, you know what we could all do?" she went on. "Play Monopoly. It's better with four people."

Patty hesitated. Monopoly *was* fun with four players. But she still couldn't picture herself making up with the twins. "What am I supposed to say?" she demanded, making a face. "I'm sorry your hair looks like yellow Brillo and I'm sorry you're so stuck up and bossy and I'm sorry I fell off your stupid bike—"

"Patty!" Mary Alice laughed, but she looked a little annoyed. "Don't make such a big thing of it. All you have to do is say you're sorry."

"I know." Patty tugged at a braid. "Well, all right," she said reluctantly. "If *they* do, I will."

Mary Alice looked up. "Here they come now! Okay, Patty. As soon as they get here, just do it and get it over with."

Together, they watched the twins bounce up the curb onto the Kallmeyers' walk and jump down from their bicycles.

Mary Alice poked Patty. "Go on."

Patty made herself walk up to the twins.

"Hi," she mumbled.

"Hi." The twins stared at her, waiting.

Patty drew a breath. "I'm sorry for what I said yesterday," she began. "And I do still want to be in the club—" she paused. "If you still want me to be."

"Sure." Myrna smiled faintly. "It would be too bad to waste the whole initiation."

Aware of Mary Alice watching from the steps, Patty held back a retort.

"I'm sorry you fell off the bike," Erna said carefully. "Is your leg okay?"

Patty nodded. "Is your bike okay?"

Myrna nodded.

For a minute, nobody said anything. Then all three of them started in at once. "Well—"

They looked at each other and laughed.

"So, let's be Special Pals again," Erna said. She put an arm around Myrna and Patty, and pulled them toward the porch.

Patty hopped into step, smiling happily at Mary Alice. That hadn't been bad at all!

"Let's play Monopoly, you guys," Mary Alice said right away. She looked over their shoulders. "Hey, guess who's coming?"

Donald Barnes was crossing the street. He came up the walk past Patty and the twins.

"Mary Alice, do you know if your sister's home?"

"Sure, I know." Mary Alice stared at him coolly.

Donald Barnes looked annoyed. "Well, would you please call her?"

Mary Alice went to the door. "Jeannie!" she called. "Your boyfriend wants you!"

With an exasperated look, Donald went inside.

Mary Alice made a face at his back. "I'll go in and get the Monopoly."

Patty and the twins threw themselves onto the glider, giggling.

Suddenly, Patty remembered her news. "Guess what?" She sat up straight. "Grandma won twenty-five dollars!"

"Wow!" Myrna said. "What for?"

"In a contest," Patty said. "She made up a name for a new kind of flour: Golden Crust. They're going to print it on every single bag they sell! And listen," she hurried on. "She's giving me two whole dollars of it. So we can spend it at Isaly's and the dime store and everything."

"Hey, that's swell!" Erna said. "Thanks, Patty."

"Guess what else?" Patty went on proudly. "Last night, I was practically riding on my bike."

"You were?" Myrna looked surprised. "Gee, if you can learn on *that*, you can ride anything, Patty."

"I know." Patty tried not to sound smug. "But when I learn, I won't *want* to ride anything except my Imperial. Imperials are the fastest."

Mary Alice came out with the Monopoly box. "You should see them in there!" she reported. "They're sitting on the couch like two lovebirds."

Erna put her hand over her heart. "Ooh, *Donald!*" she cried.

"Ooh, *Jeannie!*" Myrna fell onto her in a hug. "Please let me kiss your red ruby lips!"

"Hers are more like orange Popsicles!" Patty said as they all laughed.

Erna scrambled onto her knees and put her head

against the shaded window. "I wish we could see them."

"You know what?" Myrna suggested. "I bet if we went away for a while they'd come out here and sit, and we could sneak back and spy on them!"

"What about Monopoly?" asked Mary Alice.

"We can play later," Erna said. "*I* know!" She grabbed Patty. "Let's go over to your house and watch you ride."

Patty pulled back. Why had she boasted about it? She wasn't ready to show them yet. What if she got on and fell right off again, in front of them? She searched for an excuse. "I can't," she said. "I'm not supposed to practice till my aunt comes home."

"This wouldn't be *practicing*," said Myrna. "Just you showing us what you can do, until Jeannie and Donald come outside."

"And we'll make a lot of noise going over, so they know we've gone," Erna said, standing up.

Patty looked pleadingly at Mary Alice.

Mary Alice ignored the look.

"Come on, Patty, you *said* you could practically ride. Don't you want to *really* do it? Or are you going to spend the whole rest of the summer just watching the rest of the club ride?"

Patty stood up reluctantly. "Okay. Let's go."

"Wait a sec." Myrna went to the door. "*Come on, you kids,*" she said in a loud voice, as though they were deaf. "*Let's go over to Patty's.*"

"*Okay!*" Erna shouted, thumping down the steps.

Mary Alice and Myrna thumped down after her. *"Come on, Patty!"* Myrna yelled.

"I'm coming," Patty said, walking slowly down the steps and following them across the lawn to her yard.

Myrna pushed the bicycle toward her. *"Get on, Patty,"* she yelled. "Okay," she said in a normal tone. "Now they know we're over here. They'll probably come out on the porch in a minute. Go on, Patty. Get up. I'll hold you." She looked thoughtfully at the bicycle. "Boy, this thing *is* big. I don't blame you for being scared of it."

"I'm *not* scared of it!" Defiantly, Patty climbed up, grabbing the handlebars tightly and setting her feet on the pedals. "Go ahead," she told Myrna. "Push."

Myrna gave a small push. The bike began to roll.

"Wait!" Mary Alice grabbed the seat. "I'll hold on, too."

Patty clenched her teeth, hanging on.

Behind her, Myrna pushed again. The bike moved faster, wobbling, as the girls ran with it.

Patty looked ahead. The street was empty. "Keep going," she said, pedaling faster, as they pushed her down the curb.

Patty straightened the wheel. "Faster!" she yelled, pumping harder.

Mary Alice ran beside her, hanging on. "Stop pushing, Myrna," she panted. "Let her just pedal."

The bike swerved as Myrna let go. "Keep pumping," Mary Alice shouted. "Harder!"

The pedals circled under Patty's feet, pushing the

bike ahead in a firm, straight path. Patty bent over the handlebars, pumping furiously. The bike went smoothly on. They were almost at the Engles'! From the corner of her eye, Patty saw Buddy sitting on the steps.

"Let *go*, Mary Alice!" she cried.

There was a lurch as Mary Alice dropped back, but Patty kept right on.

"Whoopee!" Buddy yelled, waving. "Ride 'em, cowgirl!"

Patty shot past him, going straight and fast. She was *riding*! She felt the air on her face. Her braids bounced against her neck as she pumped on, breathlessly. She was almost at the corner! Now she had to slow down. Clutching the handlebars, she braked smoothly, steering the bicycle into a wide, smooth arc. For just a second, she put a foot down to steady herself. Then, taking a breath, she pedaled back up the street, past Buddy, toward the cheering girls.

Mary Alice grabbed the bike as she brought it to a stop in front of them. "You did it!"

The twins helped her get down, thumping her on the back.

Patty stood giddily on the curb. "Boy!" she gasped out, catching her breath. "Did you see me? I was *riding*!"

"I thought you might fall, you were going so fast!" Myrna said.

"I know, but I didn't!" Patty said happily. "Once I got started, I just kept going. It wasn't even that hard. Boy!" she said, hardly believing it. "I can ride!" She patted the bicycle seat. "Want to watch me do it again?"

"Wait! Let me go see if Jeannie and Donald came out yet." Myrna dashed off toward the Kallmeyers'.

"You were really good, Patty," Erna said generously. "The first time I rode alone, I fell off."

"Yeah, well, Imperials are really steady." Patty twisted around to look at the back of her legs. They felt awfully stiff. It was probably from all that pedaling.

Myrna came running back. "They're on the porch! I heard them!"

"Let's go." Erna took the bike from Patty's hands and parked it by the steps. "You can ride all day tomorrow," she said. "Where are we going to hide, Mary Alice?"

"In the bushes," Mary Alice said. "We'll sneak around the side of the house and crawl in between the bushes and the porch. Come on!" She started across the grass.

The twins hurried after her.

Patty stood where she was, looking at her bicycle.

I can ride! she told herself happily. Any time I want to, I can ride! She rubbed her leg, wishing it didn't feel so funny.

"Patty, come on." Myrna ran back for her.

"Shh!" Erna turned, putting a finger to her lips. "Don't let them hear us."

Mary Alice waited till they came up to her. Then she crouched down and squeezed into the narrow space between the lilac bushes and the porch. Erna crouched in after her, pushing branches out of her way.

"How can we *all* get in there?" Patty whispered to Myrna. "There isn't room."

"Yes, there is." Myrna nudged her forward. "Squat way down and stay near the wall."

Patty stooped low and ducked under the branches, moving awkwardly toward Erna. A branch snapped back.

"Shh!" Erna pointed upward, giggling.

Patty could hear Jeannie and Donald Barnes talking above their heads. "This is crazy!" she whispered, creeping closer to Erna. In front of them, Mary Alice moved stealthily on.

Myrna shoved in behind Patty. "Keep going," she whispered. "I can't move."

"I can't either!" Patty inched forward. This was as bad as the initiation, and a lot more uncomfortable. "I'm suffocating!" she said in Erna's ear, feeling the sweat break out on her forehead. Prickles were running up and down her legs. She reached back to rub a leg and poked Myrna by mistake.

"Hey!" Myrna lost her balance and fell against a bush. Patty reached out to pull her up.

"What was that?" they heard Jeannie ask.

"Shh!" Erna ducked low.

"What was what?" Donald's feet thumped down.

"I thought I heard some noise," Jeannie said. The glider creaked as she stood up.

Erna put her hand over her mouth, shaking with laughter.

106

"Where did those kids go, anyway?" Jeannie asked. "I thought I heard them go next door, but I don't see them now." Her feet came closer to the edge of the porch.

Myrna poked Patty.

"Who cares where they went?" Donald said, standing just above their heads. "It's a relief to get rid of them."

Mary Alice raised her arm and shook her fist in his direction.

Erna and Myrna let out little gasps of surpressed laughter. But Patty was squeezed in too tightly to laugh. Anyway, she didn't feel like laughing. She felt hot and dizzy, as though she was going to faint. Her heart was beating hard. And her legs—she tried to shift her balance—her legs felt so *prickly*.

A horrible thought flashed into her mind.

"I'm getting out!" she gasped, pushing herself awkwardly to her feet.

"*Patty!*" Myrna whispered. "Get down!"

"What's going on?" Jeannie stared angrily over the railing. "Mary *Alice*! What are you kids doing there? Donald, look! Those little twerps have been spying on us!"

"Patty, what's the matter?" Myrna stood up, staring at her anxiously.

"Of all the nerve!" Donald said, looking down. "Don't you kids have any respect?"

"Let me *out*." Patty pushed Myrna ahead of her, out of the bushes.

Erna and Mary Alice came crawling out behind

107

them. "What's wrong?" Mary Alice stared at Patty.

"I'm telling *Mama*!" Jeannie shrieked. The screen door slammed.

Patty looked at Mary Alice and the twins. "I don't feel good," she choked out. "I think I'm getting sick."

The word she couldn't say pounded in her brain, loud as her heartbeat. *Polio.*

❊
TWELVE

Patty woke in the dark, rubbing her legs against the sheet. She rolled onto her side, trying to get away from the ache and the burning itch. Her face was wet with sweat. Something awful was wrong with her.

Then she remembered.

She let out a little cry, burying her face in the damp pillow so no one would hear. What's going to happen to me? she asked herself helplessly, flinging her legs out and drawing them back in an agony of itching. Was this her awful punishment for wishing polio on the twins?

She wiped her eyes on the pillow slip, imagining Grandma and Aunt May crying over her tomorrow, when the doctor came. They would call Mom and Dad, and Aunt Flo. They would take her to the hospital, where more doctors would poke at her legs. Then they would tell her. You are paralyzed, they would say. You must lie in your bed forever. You will never walk again, and never, never ride your bicycle. . . .

Patty moaned, scratching desperately at her legs.

109

Prickles ran from her knees to her behind. Would it itch like this forever? She wondered why no one had mentioned this symptom when they talked about polio.

Tears filled her eyes as she pictured Mary Alice crying at her bedside. "Oh, Patty," she'd say, "how can you bear it?" And the twins would come crying, wishing they had never acted mean or stuck-up, even for a minute. They would fall on their knees to apologize.

"I forgive you," Patty told them bravely in her mind, rubbing her legs on the edge of the bed as she imagined the twins' shocked faces. "It doesn't matter now."

Nothing would matter! Patty stared into the dark, trying to imagine being paralyzed. You couldn't walk to school, or to Isaly's—not even to the bathroom! You couldn't run under sprinklers or sit on seesaws or jump rope. You couldn't *ride*.

Patty flopped over, wondering how she could wait till morning for help, and wishing at the same time that morning would never come. How would she tell Grandma?

She had managed not to let on yesterday.

"My stomach hurts," she had said when Grandma came home. "I don't want any supper."

"Why, Patty!" Grandma had hurried her upstairs to bed. "You and the girls must have eaten too many of those date bars for lunch. If you still feel bad in the morning," she said, feeling Patty's forehead, "I'm going to call the doctor to look at you."

Patty had turned her head away. And later, when Aunt May tiptoed into the room, she had pretended to be asleep.

Now she turned restlessly and stared at the window. The sky had brightened a little. Morning was coming. Far away, the lonesome whistle of a freight train pierced the silence. Mr. Swenson! Patty thought. What would he say if he knew what had happened to her? The train rumbled slowly through Clearwater. Patty closed her eyes and drifted into a fretful sleep, dreaming of Mr. Swenson. He was bending over a mountain stream. A silver fish, flashing in the sunlight, arced into his skillet. . . .

The sunlight woke her. She sat up and swung her prickly legs over the bed. Holding her breath, she lifted the back of her nightgown and looked down at them. She had to tell Grandma! Terrified, she limped downstairs.

Grandma and Aunt May looked up together.

"Here she is," said Aunt May cheerfully. "Do you—"

Patty threw herself at Grandma. "Grandma," she choked out. "Does polio give you a rash?"

Grandma jumped up. "Where is it, honey?" She led Patty to the window. "Oh, May," she said. "Come and look! This child has a terrible case of poison ivy!"

"Poison *ivy!*" Patty grabbed Grandma in relief. "Oh, Grandma, I thought it was polio!"

Grandma hugged her. "You poor child. You must have made yourself sick with the worry."

Aunt May held the nightgown up. "Oh, my

goodness— Why, it looks as though you sat right down in it, Patty. Where have you been?"

As soon as she asked, Patty knew. "In the Kallmeyers' side lot!" she said, scratching her leg as the itch rose up. "Mary Alice and the twins made me go in there," she added resentfully.

"Don't scratch it, Patty," Aunt May said quickly. "I'll go get some calamine lotion to put on it. That'll take the itch away." She smiled sympathetically from the doorway. "I'm afraid you won't be able to sit down for a few days."

"Boy!" Patty stared at her bike through the window. "I won't be able to ride, Grandma." Quickly, she corrected herself. "To *learn* to ride." If only she could tell Grandma that she'd done it!

"There's lots worse things could happen than that," Grandma said. "Just think how we'd feel if you did have the polio." She shook her head sadly. "I just feel so bad for those poor little children—"

"I know." Patty said, remembering her terrible nighttime fears. How could she feel sorry for herself, even with this awful itch, when some kids couldn't even *walk*?

"Come in here, Patty," Aunt May called from the living room. "I'll put the lotion on."

Patty went in and lay face down on the couch. Aunt May knelt beside her and began to dab the cool lotion onto her burning legs.

"That feels good," Patty said gratefully. "Guess what, Aunt May?" she burst out, suddenly unable to hold it back. "Do you know what I did yesterday, when you weren't home?" She lowered her voice so Grandma wouldn't hear. "I rode my bike!" Quickly she added, "I was careful. Mary Alice and the twins were with me."

"Why, Patty, isn't that wonderful!" Aunt May squeezed her arm. "I knew you could do it!" She smiled. "I guess you take after me, wanting to learn so badly that you did it on the sly." She smiled. "I've always thought we were two of a kind." She put the cap on the bottle of lotion. "We won't tell Grandma till you're better. Isn't it a pity—now you won't be *able* to ride for a while. But what an exciting thing to look forward to!"

The phone rang in the kitchen. "It's for you, Patty," Grandma called. Patty walked stiffly into the kitchen.

"Guess what, Patty," Myrna said over the phone. "I have—"

"Poison *ivy*!" Patty knew right away. "I have it, too, Myrna! Isn't it awful? Where's yours?"

Myrna gave an embarrassed laugh. "On my legs," she said. "And there's a little bit on my behind," she added.

"Me, *too*!" Patty burst out. "I can't even sit down!"

"Neither can I!" Myrna laughed. "Oh, Patty, I could just die." Her voice turned serious. "You know what I thought at first? I thought it might be *polio*."

"So did I," Patty said. "I was really scared last night." She hesitated for a minute. "Oh, Myrna, I felt so awful about what I said—"

"It's okay," said Myrna quickly. "I wasn't worried long. My legs felt funny this morning, but I showed

113

Erna and she knew what it was right away. Listen, Patty—" She giggled. "What are we going to *do* till it's over? We'll have to stand up the whole time."

"I know," Patty said. "And we can't even go riding— Hey, why don't you and Erna come over today?" she asked. "You could lie on the couch."

"I can't," Myrna said. "Mom wants me to rest at home today, and Erna said she'd stay with me. But probably tomorrow we could. Mom's getting me a new paper-doll book. I could bring it over."

"That'll be good," Patty said. Her legs had started to itch again. "I'll see you. Remember—don't scratch!" She put the phone down.

"Patty," Grandma said. "Here's someone to see you."

Mary Alice, looking solemn, came in the back door. She stared anxiously at Patty.

"Are you okay?"

"She has the poison ivy something terrible," Grandma said.

"Oh, boy," Mary Alice said. "Where do you have it?"

"On my legs," Patty said. She grinned sheepishly. "And on my behind."

"You do?" Mary Alice giggled. "Can you sit down?"

"Not really," Patty admitted.

"Patty," Grandma said, "why don't you take Mary Alice into the front room for a nice visit? My land, you didn't get your breakfast, hon. I'll bring you something on a tray."

"Thanks, Grandma."

Patty led Mary Alice to the living room. "Guess what? Myrna has it, too!"

"In the same place?" Mary Alice grinned.

"Yeah." Patty lay down on the couch. "It isn't funny, either, Mary Alice," she said. "*You* wouldn't like it if your legs were all burning and itchy and you couldn't even scratch."

"I know," said Mary Alice. "I'm sorry, Patty."

"You ought to be," Patty went on. "Know where I got it? In your side yard, doing that stupid Siam trick."

Mary Alice looked embarrassed. "Boy. I didn't know there was ivy there, honest. I thought Jeannie was just kidding." She broke off. "Hey, you should have heard Jeannie yesterday. Was she mad! So was Mom. So was Donald Barnes!" She laughed. "I heard him telling Jeannie how awful we were. I bet *he* won't come around for a while."

"Too bad on him!" Patty said. "He's a dope!"

Grandma came in with a tray. "I'll put this right here on the table, where you can reach it easy."

"Thanks, Grandma." Patty picked up a piece of toast. "So, Mary Alice," she said, biting into it. "What do you want to do?"

"We could play Monopoly," Mary Alice suggested. "Put the board on the table, and I'll sit on the floor—"

"Yeah, let's." Awkwardly, Patty drank a swallow of milk. "Go get it now, while I'm eating."

Mary Alice went out the front door. By the time Patty's toast was finished, she was back. She carried the tray to the kitchen, and opened the Monopoly board.

"What do you want?" she asked.

"The battleship." Patty raised herself up on her elbow, trying to ignore her itching legs. Except for them, this was nice. A whole long day to play Monopoly, and Mary Alice all to herself.

"Hey, Mary Alice," she said suddenly, remembering a joke she'd saved up to tell, long before she came. "What part of the body is the *yet*?"

Mary Alice looked up from the Monopoly money. "I don't know. What?"

"I don't know either," Patty said, grinning. "But this article in the paper said that a woman was shot by a bullet and they haven't got it out of her yet!"

"I don't get it." Mary Alice looked puzzled. "There's no part of you called that."

Patty wriggled happily on the couch. "That's the whole *point*!"

Mary Alice smiled uncertainly. "I get it," she said, dealing out the money.

Patty picked up the dice, and the game began.

It was still going on when Grandma brought in sandwiches for lunch, and it went on all afternoon, from the time Aunt May put lotion on Patty and went out to the Club till the time she came back and put it on again.

They were counting up their money and properties when Mary Alice jumped up. "It's Orphan Annie time!"

She turned on the radio, and the rich voice of Pierre André, Annie's special announcer, rang out. "Hello,

Orphan Annie Fans! Ready for another exciting adventure with Annie and her friends?"

Patty settled into a comfortable position on the couch, waiting.

"What's going to happen to Annie today, do you suppose?" Pierre André went on. "Well, until it's time to find out, let me ask you this: What's happening to *you* these days? Are you having lots of adventures?"

"Yes, I am," Mary Alice answered back, folding her legs under her.

"Me, too," said Patty fervently.

If Pierre André only knew! Getting poison ivy, for one thing. Learning to ride! Being in a club. Mr. Swenson! Meeting Mr. Swenson had been a *real* adventure. She'd even learned a secret code from him—a better one than Annie ever had.

Patty wriggled into a new position. She wondered how Mr. Swenson's adventure was going to turn out. If only it could have a happy ending, the way Annie's always did. But in real life, you couldn't make *everything* happen the way you wanted it to. Patty crossed her fingers. Sometimes you just had to hope.

THIRTEEN

"Vanilla, please."

Patty twisted her legs around the base of the stool and put her elbows on Isaly's cool marble counter, watching the counterman set four tall soda glasses into silver holders.

"Boy, am I thirsty!" she said happily.

"Me, too." Mary Alice swiveled on the stool beside her. "Going fast like that really makes you hot."

Myrna nudged Patty. "I can hardly *sit*!" she whispered. "Riding that far made it start itching again."

"I know it." Patty shifted uncomfortably.

It was the club's first trip downtown together on bikes. For one whole week she and Myrna had stayed close to home. Most of that time, they hadn't sat down. They had stood up to talk and knelt to cut out paper dolls, and when Mary Alice and Erna rode up and down Elm Street on their bikes, they had lain on the grass, watching.

With Myrna for company it hadn't been so bad. But near the end—when her ivy was drying up—there had been times when Patty thought she could hardly bear not being able to climb onto her bicycle seat and ride off wherever she wanted to, fast and easy and free.

It was so wonderful to know how!

Patty had written Mom and Dad to say that she had learned, and to tell them about the poison ivy. A letter had come back this very morning. "I'm so sorry to hear about your poison ivy," Mom had written. "But isn't it wonderful news that you can ride!"

"Just think, kid," Dad had added in a P.S. "In less than two weeks I'll be coming back to Clearwater for you. Maybe I'll see you riding up Elm Street to meet me!"

Two weeks! Patty had been astonished. It seemed as though the real part of her visit was just beginning. She could hardly bear to think of leaving Clearwater, and Mary Alice, and the twins.

Still, it would be awfully exciting to drive home with her bicycle strapped to the top of the car, where everyone they passed could see it. And wait till she rode it to school and showed the kids back home how fast an Imperial could go!

"I scream, you scream," the counter man said, setting their sodas in front of them.

"I'm paying for everybody." Patty pulled the money from her pocket.

"Hey, you guys." Mary Alice leaned across Patty to the twins. "Want to hear a good joke? What part of the body is the yet?"

"I think I heard that one in Columbus," Erna said. "But I don't exactly remember it."

119

"I don't know," Myrna said.

"Well, I don't know either," said Mary Alice happily. "But this article in the newspaper said a lady got shot by a bullet and they still didn't get it out of her!"

She waited for the twins' response.

"I don't get it," Erna said.

"Mary *Alice*!" Patty poked her, laughing. "You got it mixed up! Here's the way it's supposed to go—"

She began to tell the joke over, noticing happily, through Isaly's window, that her bicycle, streamlined and elegant, stood taller than all the rest.

People Called Me A Nut

"My book is not the kind that tells 'How Tomboy Mindy discovered that growing up gracefully can be as fun as playing baseball.'

"I have often thought how relaxing it would be to be invisible. But when I took over Richard's paper route they said 'girls can't deliver papers.' And when I wanted to take tennis instead of slimnastics, they said 'girls like to do graceful feminine things.' So I had to speak out. I only wanted things to be fair.

"My book is for anyone who might want to read about the life and thoughts of a person like me. If some boy wants to read this, go ahead. Maybe you will learn something."

The Real Me
by Betty Miles

An AVON CAMELOT BOOK
00347-3 • $2.50

Avon Camelot Books are available at your bookstore. Or, you may use Avon's special mail order service. Please state the title and code number and send with your check or money order for the full price, plus $1.00 per copy to cover postage and handling, to: AVON BOOK MAILING SERVICE, P.O. Box 690, Rockville Centre, NY 11571

Please allow 6-8 weeks for delivery.

AVON CAMELOT'S
FUN-FILLED FAVORITES BY

BARBARA PARK

"Park writes about youngsters in a way that
touches reality, but makes the reader double
over with laughter."

Chicago Sun-Times

SKINNYBONES
64832-6/$2.25
The story of a Little League player with a big league
mouth.

OPERATION: DUMP THE CHUMP
63974-2/$2.25
Oscar's little brother is a creep, but Oscar has a
plan...

DON'T MAKE ME SMILE
61994-6/$2.50 US/$2.95 Can
Charlie Hinkle has decided to live in a tree—
and nothing can make him give up his fight!

Buy these books at your local bookstore or use this coupon for ordering:

AVON BOOK MAILING SERVICE, P.O. Box 690, Rockville Centre, NY 11571
Please send me the book(s) I have checked above. I am enclosing $ _____
(please add $1.00 to cover postage and handling for each book ordered to a
maximum of three dollars). *Send check or money order*—no cash or C.O.D.'s
please. Prices and numbers are subject to change without notice. Please allow six
to eight weeks for delivery.

Name _____

Address _____

City _____ State/Zip _____

PARK 10/85